WITHDRAWN

The Glittering Lights

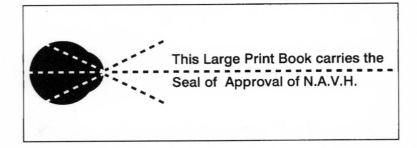

This Large Print Book carries the
Seal of Approval of N.A.V.H.

The Glittering Lights

Barbara Cartland

Thorndike Press • Thorndike, Maine

Published in 2001 by arrangement with
International Book Marketing Limited.

Thorndike Press Large Print Candlelight Series.

The tree indicium is a trademark of Thorndike Press.

The text of this Large Print edition is unabridged.
Other aspects of the book may vary from the original edition.

Set in 16 pt. Plantin by Susan Guthrie.

Printed in the United States on permanent paper.

Library of Congress Cataloging-in-Publication Data
Cartland, Barbara, 1902–
    The glittering lights / Barbara Cartland.
      p.   cm.
    ISBN: 0-7862-3136-X (lg. print : hc : alk. paper)
    1. Inheritance and succession — Fiction. 2. London
(England) — Fiction. 3. Music-halls — Fiction. 4. Large
type books. I. Title.
PR6005.A765 G57 2001
823'.912—dc21   00-053624

AUTHOR'S NOTE

The background of this novel is authentic; the descriptions and gossip about the beautiful Lily Langtry, the Show at the Gaiety Theatre and its pretty Leading Ladies, the restaurants in London like Romanos, Rules, the Café Royal are all part of the history of the time.

Chapter One

1886

"I am back, Mama."

"Oh, Cassandra, I have been so worried! You are very late!"

"I had trouble with one of the horses," Cassandra said walking across the Drawing-Room to where her mother was sitting in a wheel-chair in front of the fire.

As she reached her, Lady Alice Sherburn looked up and gave an exclamation of horror.

Her daughter was certainly looking most disreputable. Her habit was splashed with mud, her hair had escaped from beneath her riding-hat, and she also appeared to be extremely wet.

Cassandra saw her mother's face and gave a little laugh.

"I am safe and sound," she said reassuringly, "but wet through! It is raining and I had a fall."

"Cassandra!"

The cry was one of horror.

Reaching her mother's side, Cassandra leaned down and kissed her cheek.

"Now do not worry, Mama, about something which has not happened. It was not a bad fall, and although I may be a little stiff tomorrow, there are no bones broken, and not too many bruises . . . not where they will show, anyway!"

"Cassandra, my dearest, if anything happened to you, I do not think I could bear it."

"I know that, Mama," Cassandra said in a soft voice, "and that is why I came in to tell you I was back before I went upstairs to change. Otherwise I would not have let you see me looking like this."

She saw the fear still lurking in her mother's eyes and said quietly:

"You know lightning never strikes in the same place twice! You have taken all the dangers of the family upon yourself, so Papa and I are likely to get off scot-free."

"If only you were not so reckless," Lady Alice murmured almost beneath her breath.

Cassandra kissed her mother's cheek once again.

"There is nothing you and Papa would dislike more than if I were a mouse-like little Miss, sitting at home with my tatting," she said. "And you, as one of the best horse-women the County ever saw, would disown a daughter who trit-trotted along the roads and looked for gaps in the hedges."

Lady Alice smiled.

"I cannot imagine you ever being that kind of rider! Go and change, child, and when you are looking decent your father wants to see you."

"He will have to wait a little while," Cassandra replied airily. "I must have a bath, and while I am about it, I shall put on my evening-gown. So tell Papa, if he asks for me, it will be at least an hour before he can expect me."

"I will send a message to your father," Lady Alice replied. "Cassandra, I. . . ."

But her daughter had already left the room and was running up the broad stairway to her own bed-room.

Her maid, Hannah, was waiting for her there and, like Lady Alice, she gave an exclamation of horror at Cassandra's appearance.

"Now do not start screaming at me," Cassandra admonished with a smile. "I took a toss this afternoon. It was all my fault. I tried a young horse at too high a fence and he refused at the last moment."

"You'll break your neck one of these days, Miss Cassandra," Hannah said in the scolding voice of an old servant whose affection allows her to take liberties.

Cassandra did not answer and she went on:

"And I should have thought that seeing your mother every day in her wheel-chair would be a warning to you. But no, you ride as if the devil himself was at your heels! But one day, you'll get what's coming to you."

Cassandra gave a little sigh.

She had heard all this before. At the same time, she understood her mother's anxiety and Hannah's.

For the last fifteen years, Lady Alice had been confined to a wheel-chair, having broken her back out hunting.

Yet, surprisingly, it had drawn she and her husband closer together.

There had never been, people said, a more devoted, considerate man than Sir James Sherburn, and Lady Alice's love for him was very evident every time her eyes rested on his handsome face.

The real tragedy lay in the fact that because of her incapacity they could have no more children.

Cassandra, who was five at the time of her mother's accident, was their only child.

That she was lovely, daring, reckless, and impulsive was to be expected in the offspring of two such attractive and unusual people, and Cassandra had certainly lived up to their expectations of her.

To begin with, she was startlingly beautiful.

As Hannah took off her dirty riding-habit, she stood for a moment naked before stepping into her bath which was waiting in front of the fire.

The perfection of her slender figure with its white skin made her look like a young goddess.

She released her hair from the last remaining pins that had not been dislodged while riding, and it fell over her shoulders reaching nearly to her waist.

It was a colour which drew every man's eyes when she entered a room. Deep red, it was highlighted with streaks of gold which appeared to ripple through it and shine tantalisingly, so that no-one was able exactly to describe it.

Cassandra's hair was a heritage from her father and he often said that 'red hair ran like wine' in the Sherburn family.

But she had her mother's eyes and Lady Alice came from a long line of Irish nobility.

The O'Derrys had been Earls of Ireland for generations, and it was always said that the dark lashes which framed their blue eyes were a legacy from a Spanish ancestor.

He had, according to legend, been swept up on the South coast of Ireland from one of the wrecked galleons of the Spanish Armada and had married the pretty daughter of his captor.

The combination of red hair and blue eyes made Cassandra inevitably the object of attention.

It would have been a blind man who could resist the enticement of her smile or the way her laugh would ring out making everyone want to laugh with her.

She was naturally gay, invariably happy, and an irrepressible mad-cap which made some older members of Yorkshire society raise their eye-brows and look down their aristocratic noses.

But even they had to admit that Cassandra was irresistible, and they forgave her escapades which would have brought down the full weight of their disapproval on any other girl.

"I have had a really marvelous day," Cassandra said as having washed herself she lay back in the bath, feeling her stiffness ease away in the warm water.

She thought with satisfaction of the results she had obtained with the young horses her father had bought for her the previous week.

There was not another girl in the whole of Yorkshire who could have attempted to school her own mounts or to ride them over what was in effect a private steeple-chase course in the grounds of her own home.

"By the time hunting starts," she said, talking more to herself than to Hannah, "I shall have horses with which I shall out-ride and out-stay anyone else in the field."

"You'll do that — if you're alive to tell the tale!" Hannah said tartly.

She went from the room as she spoke, carrying the muddied and wet habit with her.

Cassandra laughed to herself.

She was used to Hannah fussing over her, but it hurt her if she knew her mother was anxious. That was why she had hurried in to see Lady Alice before she went upstairs to change.

At twenty Cassandra had lost her last remnants of adolescent awkwardness and to a great degree her shyness.

She was usually very sure of herself, and she would have been stupid — which she was not — if she had not been conscious of her own attractions.

There was hardly a young man in the whole neighbourhood who had not pursued her ardently and incessantly.

While she laughed at them for being immature, she was well aware there was a glint in the eyes of her father's old acquaintances when they looked at her and that the compliments they paid her were, for the most part, sincere.

"Thank goodness we are not dining out tonight," she thought as she stepped out of the bath.

The Sherburns lived in a very hospitable neighbourhood despite the fact that on the map it appeared somewhat isolated.

It was, however, excellent hunting country and that was what mattered, combined with the good fortune of having a large number of young people among the families of the big landowners.

When Cassandra finished drying herself, Hannah was ready to help her into one of the exquisite gowns on which her father was only too happy to spend exorbitant sums.

Naturally they came from London and were the source of considerable envy, and sometimes a little malice, amongst the other girls of Cassandra's age.

But it was difficult for anyone to resent her for long.

She was as charming to women as she was to men, and apart from her shocking the older generation by behaving more like a boy than a girl in the hunting field and at other sports, there was no denying that she had been very properly brought up.

14

"Thank you, Hannah," she said now as she finished dressing. "Be an angel and call me at 7 o'clock tomorrow morning."

"You're not going riding at that unearthly hour!" Hannah exclaimed. "Not after you've been out so late today."

"I am not going to let my horses forget what I have already taught them," Cassandra replied, "and tomorrow I will get Flycatcher to jump that fence I am sure of it!"

"You're tempting Providence, that's what you're doing," Hannah said warningly.

But Cassandra only laughed at her once again.

"If I break my neck, it will give you so much satisfaction to say — 'I told you so,' " she teased.

With her gown making a silky swish behind her she went down the stairs towards her father's Study.

She stepped into the room and he looked up from his desk, appreciating with the eyes of a man who was a connoisseur of beautiful women how lovely she looked.

Her dress was the pale leaf green of the spring buds that were just beginning to show on the trees, and a skilful hand had molded it over the front of her body so that it revealed the perfect contours of her breasts and her tiny waist.

It was almost Classical in its simplicity to fall from the bustle in a cascade of frills which ended in a small train.

It was the dress of a young girl and yet every line proclaimed it to have been extremely expensive.

Cassandra wore no jewellery: with her white skin that had the texture of a magnolia she needed none.

Her hair was swept back from her oval forehead and because she had been in a hurry, Hannah had simply arranged it in a large chignon rather than in the multiple curls which Sir James preferred.

But whichever way Cassandra wore her unusual and beautiful hair, it was always spectacular.

"I am sorry if I kept you waiting, Papa," she said as she walked across the large room and lifted up her face for him to kiss her.

"I forgive you," he replied.

When they were together, the likeness between father and daughter was very obvious, despite the fact that Cassandra was small-boned with delicate very feminine features, and Sir James was a handsome very masculine man.

He was dressed with an elegance which accentuated the lean and athletic lines of his figure.

His clean-cut features, his eyes which seemed to have a permanent twinkle in them, and his ability to make the most outrageous flattering compliments sound sincere, rendered him irresistible to women.

"I wish you had been with me, Papa," Cassandra exclaimed. "Those horses are outstanding! I cannot tell you how excited I am by their performance."

"I am glad they please you," Sir James said.

"You know they do," Cassandra answered, "and I think we have a real winner in Andora."

"I seldom make a mistake when it comes to horseflesh," Sir James murmured.

Cassandra walked towards the fire.

It was the end of March, but the weather was still very chill and The Towers was a cold house, being not only very large but built on the summit of a hill with magnificent views over the surrounding countryside.

"Mama was worried because I was late," Cassandra said.

"I know," Sir James answered. "Try not to upset her, my dearest."

"I do try," Cassandra answered, "but Flycatcher threw me. I had to school him for at least half an hour afterwards — otherwise he would have thought he could get away with it."

Sir James, who had followed Cassandra to the fireplace, smiled at her gently.

"I think you now are as proficient with horses as I am and quite frankly, I could not pay you a bigger compliment."

"I would not like to suggest that you sound conceited," Cassandra teased. "At the same time I know that something has pleased you. What is it, apart from me?"

"You always please me," Sir James said with a note of seriousness in his voice, "but you are right as usual. There is something I have to tell you."

"What can it be?" Cassandra asked.

She had a feeling there was something unusual in the expression on her father's face.

Sir James hesitated for a moment and then he said quietly:

"I have had a letter from the Duke."

Cassandra was very still.

"I have been expecting it, as you well know," Sir James went on. "At the same time I began to feel that since he had come into the title he was no longer interested in the arrangements his father had made for him."

"It is over a year," Cassandra murmured almost beneath her breath.

"I know that," Sir James said, "and I should think it almost insulting if he had not prefixed his letter with 'Now that the period of mourning for my father has ended . . .' "

"And how does he go on?" Cassandra asked.

"He suggests that his visit here, which has been postponed for so long, should now take place," Sir James replied. "He asks if he would be welcome in two weeks time, on the tenth of April to be exact."

Cassandra turned her head away to look at the fire. She held out her hands towards the flames as if she suddenly felt cold.

Sir James looked at her profile a little while before he said:

"You know, dearest, without my having to tell you, that I have always wanted you to marry the son of my old friend. We have not spoken about it for some time, but we are both aware it has been in the back of our minds."

'That is true,' Cassandra thought.

She and her father always knew what the other was thinking and it had been obvious these past months that they both deliberately avoided the subject of her marriage.

"It was all arranged and everything appeared to be straight-forward," Sir James continued, "until everything was upset by two or should I say three, unexpected deaths."

'That also is true,' Cassandra thought.

It had been planned that she should make her *début* in the summer of 1884. She was to have gone to London and her father had planned a Ball at a house he had recently acquired in Park Lane.

She was to have been presented at Buckingham Palace and to have been chaperoned, as her mother was unable to do so, by her father's step-sister, Lady Fladbury.

Then a week before they were due to leave Yorkshire, her mother's father, the Earl of O'Derry, had died and they had been plunged into mourning.

Queen Victoria had set a precedent for mourning long and ostentatiously every relative however seldom one had met them and however slight the ties of affection.

It was therefore impossible for Cassandra to make her *début* then. All the arrangements that had been made in London were cancelled and they stayed in Yorkshire.

The following year the scene was set once again and Lady Fladbury who was only too willing to present Cassandra to London society, had actually sent out invitations to Receptions, Soirées and Balls to coincide with her arrival in London.

Two days before Cassandra and her father were due to set out from Yorkshire, Lord Fladbury died of a sudden heart-attack.

"That settles it!" Cassandra said. "I am obviously fated not to be a débutante!"

"Fladbury was only an Uncle by marriage," Sir James said, "but as the Social world knows that my step-sister was chaperoning you, we can hardly ignore the fact that she is widowed and that we must wear black for at least a month or two."

"Cassandra cannot be presented in the circumstances," Lady Alice had said in concern. "I would take her to Buckingham Palace myself, despite the fact that I am in a wheel-chair, but how can I make an application before poor George is even in the grave. It would be in the worst possible taste."

"It does not worry me in the slightest, Mama," Cassandra said. "Quite frankly I would much rather spend the summer here in Yorkshire. You know as well as I do that I enjoy the races, and I find my own friends with whom I have been brought up far more agreeable than all the strange notabilities to whom I should be very small fry."

"Dammit! I wanted you to have a London Season," Sir James said irritably, "and I have made all the arrangements with the Duke."

That, Cassandra knew, annoyed her father more than anything else.

Sir James and the Duke of Alchester had

decided many years ago that their children should marry each other.

The Duke wanted an heiress for his son — he made no bones about it! His great estate was mortgaged, the house was in disrepair, and the Marquess of Charlbury was well aware that he had to marry money.

"I had been half-afraid that I should have to put up with a damned American or a tradesman's daughter," the Duke had snorted to Sir James. "What could be better than that your girl and my boy should make a match, and we can see that they do things properly."

The Marquess of Charlbury, who was six years older than Cassandra, had been abroad when it had all been decided.

"I have sent the boy to see the world," the late Duke said. "It will make him appreciate his position in this country. No-body, as you well know, Sherburn, has a better family tree or a finer family seat. It is just that we have not enough money to keep it up."

Sir James and the Duke of Alchester had been friends for some years. They had met at Tattersall's Sale-rooms where for some months they vied against each other in trying to acquire the finest horses.

It was after Sir James had out-bid the

Duke and paid an exorbitant price for two particularly fine hunters, that he had walked up to the older man to say:

"It strikes me, Your Grace, that we are pouring a lot of unnecessary money, not only into the pockets of the owners, but also into the hands of those who run this Sale-room."

The Duke looked at Sir James in surprise. Then he had succumbed, just as so many other people had done before him, to the younger man's charm.

"What do you suggest we do about it?" he asked.

"Come to a sensible arrangement between us!" Sir James replied. "We can inspect the horses before the sales, pick out those in which we are personally interested, and agree as to which ones each shall bid for."

The same agreement applied to their race-horses. When they went to the Newmarket or to the sales which took place on the race-course, they were always seen consulting each other and if one of them was bidding the other was silent.

Because the love of horses is the closest bond that an Englishman can have with another, the Duke and Sir James Sherburn became close friends.

Cassandra was only twelve when she first saw the Marquis of Charlbury.

Her father had taken her to the Eton v. Harrow cricket match at Lords. They had a Coach on the Mound, while an innumerable number of people of all ages drank champagne and ate raspberries and cream, usually with their backs to the cricket.

Cassandra however watched the boys in their white flannels fighting the annual battle of Eton College against Harrow School, and it had been impossible not to realise that the Captain of Eton was an outstanding young man.

He took four wickets and made sixty runs and had, it appeared, ensured almost single handed, that Eton was the winner.

He had been brought by the Duke to Sir James's Coach during the afternoon and Cassandra, seated on the box, had looked down at him with interest.

She had not realised then that her future was already being planned for her by her father and the Duke.

In his long white flannel trousers, blazer and pale blue cap the Marquis had appeared extremely handsome. His hair was dark and he had grey eyes which she noticed immediately.

There was an expression of curiosity in them which made him, she thought, appear to look penetratingly at anyone to whom he spoke, as if he was searching for something.

He was tall and extremely thin, as if he had almost outgrown his strength, or else driven himself hard.

There was no doubt that he was popular with other Etonians, while older men spoke of what he had achieved at the match with a pride that told those who listened it was part of the nostalgia of their school-days.

The Duke was talking eagerly to Sir James about a horse he had heard of in Suffolk and which he thought was worth their attention.

The young Marquis was surrounded by the young women who had been accepting Sir James's hospitality.

They were flattering him, hanging on his words, laughing at everything he said and doing their utmost, Cassandra thought with a little curve of her lips, to make themselves alluring.

'Today he is the hero of the match,' she thought. 'Tomorrow they will have forgotten him.'

But she was to learn as the years went on that the Marquis of Charlbury was not someone who was easily forgotten!

The newspapers were full of him, the illustrated journals went into rhapsodies over his looks, his charm and his rank.

She could never remember afterwards whether they had actually been introduced that day at Lords.

But whether they had or not, she had certainly made no impact upon him, while she knew that as far as she was concerned her life had been changed that warm summer's afternoon.

It seemed to her inevitable and in a way part of a dream when her father told her that he and the Duke had planned that she should marry the Marquis.

"And supposing he does not like me?" she asked.

For a moment Sir James looked a little embarrassed.

"My dearest, you must understand," he said, "that in the social world marriages are arranged by the parents of those concerned."

"But could such a marriage ever be successful?" Cassandra enquired.

"They are successful," Sir James answered. "In the vast majority of cases the two people concerned fall in love with each other after the marriage and live in great contentment."

"Are you telling me that that is what happened with you and Mama?"

Sir James smiled.

"As usual, Cassandra, you have put your

finger upon my Achilles heel! I met your mother by chance. I fell in love with her as soon as I saw her. I think she will tell you that she also fell in love with me."

He paused and then he said:

"I was much older then she, Cassandra. I always intended to marry, but only when I was quite certain I found someone who would suit me."

"In other words," Cassandra said, "you meant to marry someone who had both breeding and an important place in the social world. You were rich, Papa, but you had no intention of not furthering your ambitions by your marriage."

"We have always been frank with each other," Sir James replied, "and therefore I can admit in all honesty, Cassandra, that that is more or less the truth. I had no intention, when I gave up my bachelor-hood, of making anything but a brilliant social marriage, something which I may add I had enjoyed very much."

Cassandra laughed.

"I have heard it said, Papa, that there has never been such a flirt as you, and that women pursued you like flies around a honey-pot!"

"You flatter me!" Sir James protested, but his eyes were twinkling.

"What you are trying to tell me," Cassandra went on, "is that you always intended to make a *mariage de convenance*. You would not have married someone unimportant, however much you loved her."

"I was fortunate in that the situation did not arise," Sir James said, "so I cannot tell you what I would have done in different circumstances. It was true I was enamoured with many lovely women and perhaps you are right in saying I broke a number of hearts! But the moment I saw your mother I loved her."

There was something rather moving in the simplicity with which he spoke.

"And I am not to have the same chance of finding someone I love," Cassandra said in a small voice.

Sir James made a gesture with his hands.

"My dear, you are a woman and how can a woman judge what is best for herself? Not a rich woman at any rate."

"You mean that, as soon as I am old enough, men will want to marry me for my money?" Cassandra said.

"Men will want to marry you because you are lovely, because you are sweet, intelligent and have a personality of your own," Sir James corrected. "And, to add to all that, you are also a very wealthy young woman!"

Cassandra sighed.

"So I have to allow you to choose my husband?"

"You have to trust me as you have always done, to know what is best for you."

"And what about the Marquis?" Cassandra enquired. "He is a man. He can have his own choice as you did."

"No! Charlbury has to marry for money," Sir James said. "There is no question of that. The Alchester Estate is in the red. Because I am the Duke's friend, he has confided in me that it will require a small fortune to set things to rights. The only chance Charlbury has of living in the home of his ancestors is to take a rich wife."

"He may . . . love someone quite . . . different."

Cassandra felt as though she forced the words between her lips.

"He is a gentleman," Sir James replied. "He will, I know, always show his wife courtesy and consideration. I have never heard anyone say anything unpleasant or indeed unkind about Charlbury."

Cassandra felt after this conversation that her father would arrange for her to meet the young Marquis. He so often went to stay at Alchester Park with the Duke or they met at one of their Clubs.

It seemed strange that no invitation for her came to The Towers and there was never any question of the Marquis being asked to stay for one of the innumerable Balls or functions which took place in Yorkshire.

When she was older she realised that this was deliberate on her father's part.

He did not wish the Marquis to see her when, as he put it himself, she was unfledged, half-grown, not quite as beautiful as she promised to be.

But there was no doubt they would have met when she went to London for her *début*, had not Sir James's plans been frustrated twice so that they had to remain in Yorkshire.

Then, as if fate had not finished putting obstacles in their way, the Duke died in 1885.

He had stroke when he was watching one of his horses beaten at the post Epsom racecourse and only survived for twenty-four hours.

This was even a bigger set-back than Sir James had endured previously.

He had just arranged that the young Marquis should come and stay at The Towers for the local races and to take part in the County festivities which always coincided with them.

He had not pretended to Cassandra that this was not the auspicious moment in her life.

"You will meet Charlbury, he will propose to you, and you can be married at the end of the summer."

"Does he realise what has been planned for him?" Cassandra asked.

"Of course," her father replied. "The Duke has already invited us to stay at Alchester for Ascot, and by that time your engagement will be in the 'Gazette'."

Cassandra had said very little. She felt as if she was waiting in a theatre for the curtain to rise and was not quite certain which play was being performed.

When she was alone a thousand questions came into her mind, a thousand fears and doubts and apprehensions seemed to encompass her like a cloud.

Then with the Duke's death, everything came to a standstill.

Sir James had travelled South to attend the funeral and he had not suggested that Cassandra should come with him.

Anyway she also was in mourning, and she was well aware it would not be right for her to meet her future husband at the death-bed of his father.

And so her second summer was spent in

31

Yorkshire, while Sir James, she knew, waited at first confidently and then with some degree of anxiety for a letter from the new Duke of Alchester.

Cassandra waited too and for the first time in her life, she had not confided her thoughts and feelings to her father.

They were so close that she never had any secrets that he could not share.

"Who offered for you tonight?" he would ask as they travelled back from a Ball at which Cassandra had undoubtedly been the Belle and evoked the admiration of every male and the envy of every female.

"John Huntley, for the nine hundred and ninety-ninth time," she replied laughingly. "I am fond of him, but he does not seem to understand that the word 'No' exists in the English language."

"I admire his persistence," Sir James said.

"He is as heavy-handed as a suitor as he is with a horse," Cassandra had said.

"And what could be more condemning?" Sir James remarked with a smile.

"I know one thing . . . I could never marry a man who could not ride well and did not understand horses."

"There are plenty of good riders to be found," Sir James said mockingly.

"You know I also want someone intelligent," Cassandra said, "and that is more than I can say for Walter Witley. If you had heard him stammering and hesitating tonight, you would have been really sorry for him.

"I tried to prevent him coming to the point, but he had made up his mind to 'try his luck', as he put it. But I do not think he will try again."

"Were you unkind to him?" Sir James asked curiously.

"No, but I have deflated his ego," Cassandra answered. "He thinks Lord Witley of Witley Park is too much of a catch to be turned down by the daughter of a mere Baronet!"

"Damn it all!" Sir James ejaculated. "The Sherburns were Squires in Yorkshire when the Witleys were nothing but sheep-shearers."

Cassandra had laughed.

"Oh, Papa, I love you when you are proud of your ancestry and you give the *parvenus* a set-down! But Lord Witley is Lord Witley and he never lets anyone forget it."

"Well, I will tell your mother to delete him from her list of eligible young men," Sir James said, "and quite frankly, if you married a Witley, I should refuse to come to your wedding."

Cassandra laughed again and then linking her arm in her father's she said:

"The trouble is, Papa, that I find you so fascinating, so amusing, so clever, and so unusually intelligent, that all other men pale into insignificance beside you."

Sir James kissed the top of her head.

"You spoil me, Cassandra. At the same time, as you well know, I want the best — the very best — for you, and that is what I intend you to have."

It was now that the Duke's belated letter had arrived, that Cassandra found herself for the first time questioning her father's wisdom where she was concerned.

She knew that, had the Marquis of Charlbury come to stay as had been arranged the previous year, she would have accepted his proposal as her father intended, and by now they would have been married.

'But,' she told herself, 'in the past year I have changed.'

She was not a very young girl standing on the threshold of life, a little bewildered and uncertain of herself, and unsure of what she wanted of the future.

In simple words she had grown up.

At twenty she was no longer a débutante, and because she was far more intelligent than the average girl of her age, or indeed of most women at any age, she was prepared to look critically at her suitor and not accept him just because it pleased her father.

Sir James was perceptive enough to know that something was perturbing her.

While he was confident that in due course Cassandra would tell him what it was, he also was aware that he was no longer dealing with a child who would obey him without question.

There was no time to say much more to each other. Dinner was announced and they proceeded to the Dining-Room, Lady Alice being wheeled ahead of Sir James and Cassandra.

As might be expected, the meal was superlatively cooked by a French Chef, whose salary to keep him in Yorkshire was an extravagance which few other men would have contemplated.

There were flowers decorating the Dining-Room table from the huge greenhouses which covered over two acres of garden, there were fruits forced in a manner which commanded the admiration of all the horticulturists in the North of England, and Sir James's gold racing trophies helped to decorate the table.

Sir James seated himself in his high-backed chair and remarked with satisfaction:

"How nice it is to have on either side of me two of the most beautiful women in the world, and to know that tonight I do not have to make polite conversation with a number of boring acquaintances."

Lady Alice laughed.

"You like having us alone because it is a novelty, but if it was something which occurred too often you would soon be yawning."

"How can you say anything so unkind?"

Sir James took his wife's hand and raised it to his lips.

"Have I ever appeared to be bored with you?"

"No, darling," Lady Alice answered, "but I take very good care that you have many distractions to amuse you."

It was true, Cassandra thought, watching them. Lady Alice would arrange for all the most attractive and beautiful women she knew to stay at The Towers and be their guests at luncheon, dinner and on every possible occasion.

She sometimes wondered if her mother felt jealous at the way in which they flirted outrageously with her father and obviously set themselves out to use every possible feminine allure to attract him.

Then she knew with that new instinct that she had discovered in herself that Lady Alice held her husband by not appearing to do so.

There was between them an understanding which seemed to enrich their lives, so that Cassandra knew that no-one, however beautiful, would ever take the place of her mother in his affections.

At the same time, she was well aware that Sir James had the reputation of being a Don Juan and that women found him irresistible.

"It is not surprising, Papa," she had told him once, "because I also find you irresistible and I am your daughter."

"I can return the compliment," he said, "and one day when you fall in love, Cassandra, the man to whom you give your heart will find it is possible to express your attractions in words."

When dinner was over they sat for a little while in the Drawing-Room talking in front of the fire, and then when Lady Alice went up to bed, Cassandra rose to follow her.

"I admit to feeling a little stiff, and also a trifle tired."

"Are you riding early tomorrow?" her father asked. "I think I might come with you."

Cassandra hesitated a moment before she replied:

"I think, Papa, I will go to London."

"To London?" Sir James exclaimed.

He realised that Lady Alice, being propelled towards the lift he had had installed for her, was out of earshot.

"I need some clothes, Papa."

"But of course! That is understandable. I want you to look your best, Cassandra, when Alchester arrives."

"I hope I will do that."

"Do you want me to come with you?"

"No, Papa, you know how much it would bore you if I was having fittings all day, and I do not expect I shall stay long."

"I know your Aunt is at our house in Park Lane," Sir James said. "I had a letter from her yesterday telling me she had engaged a new Cook."

The widowed Lady Fladbury had, after her husband's death, made her home in her Step-brother's house in Park Lane.

It was convenient for Cassandra if she wished to go to London at any time to have a Chaperon on the premises, and it suited her aunt, who had been left in somewhat impecunious circumstances, to live rent free.

"Aunt Eleanor never goes away!" Cassandra said. "So I was certain I would find her there."

"You will take Hannah?"

"Of course," Cassandra replied. "I know you would not like me to travel without her."

"Then the sooner you go to London and come back, the better," Sir James said, "and by the way, while you are there, have a photograph taken. We shall need it for the newspapers when your engagement is announced."

"Oh, Papa, you know I hate being photographed."

"I cannot abide the last one that was taken by that man in York," Sir James said. "I want an attractive likeness to console me when you have left home."

"Yes, of course, I had not thought of that. It would be awkward if you forgot what I looked like."

He smiled at her fondly.

"You know I could never do that. At the same time I want a very good one. Go to Downey's of Bond Street, who photographed Lily Langtry. I liked the last one I saw of her."

Cassandra was still for a moment and then she said:

"There is something I want to ask you,

Papa. I would like to meet Mrs. Langtry."

"You would?" Sir James exclaimed in surprise.

"I have heard so much about her," Cassandra replied, "of her beauty, and the sensation she caused when she went on the stage. I was reading how when she returned from America last year, she was cheered as she stepped from the ship. There were crowds of people waiting on the quay to see her."

"I read that too," Sir James said.

"It shows what a place she holds in public affection," Cassandra went on. "Write me a letter of introduction, Papa, and I will go and see her new play."

"It is called 'Enemies' and it is on at the Prince's theatre."

"Have you seen it yet?"

He shook his head.

"No. I saw the play she was in before. She was good — a little stiff — but she looked entrancingly lovely."

"Did you take her out to supper, Papa?"

"As a matter of fact, no, I did not," Sir James answered, "and, as you are so curious, I have not seen her since she returned to England from America last year."

"Then she will be looking forward to hearing from you again," Cassandra said. "Give me just a few words of introduction."

"I do not know her address. You will have to get the coachman to leave it at the theatre. At the same time, I am not really certain your mother would like you to meet an actress, even if it is Mrs. Langtry."

"We can solve that problem by not telling Mama. I expect she knows that at one time you were fascinated by the most beautiful woman in England, but she may now have forgotten all about it."

"Then we will not tell her," Sir James smiled, "and I would rather like you to meet Lily. You are as lovely in your way, Cassandra, as she is in hers."

He sighed.

"Let me think, she must be twenty nine, and when I knew her first she was only twenty two, and the most beautiful creature I ever encountered."

"You understand, Papa, why I want to meet her? I will just talk to her and see how she captivated the Prince of Wales and Prince Louis of Battenburg, and why the Prime Minister Mr. Gladstone is her friend."

"I cannot think who has been talking to you about such matters," Sir James said, but there was no reproof in his voice.

"If there is any scandal I have not yet heard," Cassandra said with a smile. "Aunt

Eleanor will be full of it as soon as I arrive in Park Lane."

"You can be quite sure of that," Sir James agreed.

"Then you had best write me a letter now," Cassandra insisted. "If I am going to London, I will catch the 9 A.M. train from York, so it will mean my leaving early.

"Will you order the carriage for me, Papa, and as soon as I go upstairs I will tell Hannah to start packing. She will be furious at having to do it at what she will call the 'middle of the night'."

"And do not worry your mother," Sir James admonished. "You know she is rather anxious when you go to London without me."

"I am sure Mama will want me to look my very best when the Duke arrives," Cassandra said demurely. "Like every woman you have ever known, Papa, I literally have not a thing to wear!"

Sir James laughed at that and walking across the room went through the Hall and into his Study.

He sat down at the desk and wrote a short note in his strong, upright handwriting and put it into an envelope.

Sir James addressed it to: "Mrs. Langtry, The Prince's Theatre".

"Thank you, dear Papa," Cassandra said and bending, kissed his cheek.

She slipped the letter inside the bodice of her dress before she went to her mother's bed-room.

She said good-night to Lady Alice, told her that she was about to go to London, and found, as she expected, that her mother apparently understood her need for more clothes.

It was Hannah who protested when Cassandra, going to her bed-room, found her there waiting to help her undress.

"Really, Miss Cassandra, you might give me a little more notice," she scolded. "How do you think I'm going to get ready by 8 o'clock tomorrow morning unless I stay up all night?"

"You know you never go to sleep early," Cassandra replied, "and it is important, Hannah, it is, really or I would not have made up my mind so unexpectedly."

"Are you up to some of your monkey tricks again?" Hannah asked. "Because if you are, you can take someone else with you. I shall not be responsible to Her Ladyship, and that's a fact!"

Cassandra paid no attention.

She had heard Hannah talk like this far too many times before to be taken seriously.

"I'll go and start packing," Hannah said when finally Cassandra was ready for bed. "It'll take me three hours. If I'm too exhausted to come with you in the morning, you'll understand what has happened."

"I have already told you, Hannah," Cassandra said, "I only want a few gowns, so do not pack half the wardrobe. I shall only be staying two or three days and I shall be shopping all the time."

"I can't think where we're going to put any more things. There's no room for what we have already," Hannah remarked as a parting shot.

As soon as she was alone, Cassandra jumped out of bed and put on the silk wrap which Hannah had left lying over a chair.

She tied the sash around her small waist and went from the bed-room into her Sitting-room which adjoined it.

It was a lovely room and had been done up only two years ago by her father who had spared no expense.

Everything that Cassandra treasured, everything that meant something special to her was housed here in the room that was essentially her own.

She lit the lamp which had been turned out by Hannah before she left and found a key in its secret drawer which was indiscernible to anyone who did not know where it was concealed.

With it she opened the lower drawer of her desk in which reposed two large green leather Albums.

She took one out and put it on the table beside the lighted lamp.

For a moment she stared at it as if she was half afraid to turn the cover with its silver edges and reveal what lay inside.

Then very slowly, with a strange expression on her face, she opened the Album.

Chapter Two

Cassandra turned the pages.

On every one there were portrait-sketches, cuttings from newspapers and magazines, all referring to the Marquis of Charlsbury.

She had started to collect newspaper reports of him after she had seen him at the Eton and Harrow match.

There had been quite glowing descriptions of the way he himself had batted and how expertly he had captained his team.

Cassandra had cut them out of the many newspapers her father read and from the *Illustrated London News*, the *Sporting and Dramatic*, and the magazines like *The Lady* which amused her mother.

Later she thought she had done it instinctively, because sub-consciously she had known even then that the Marquis was to mean something in her life.

After her father had told her that he intended her to marry the Marquis she had bought the leather Album and stuck in the cuttings.

She started with 1878 when she first met him and added to them year by year until they had stopped abruptly in August 1885.

It was not that he did not continue to haunt her dreams, to linger at the back of her mind whatever she might be doing.

It was just that she knew that, unless things were very different than they appeared to be at the moment, it would be impossible for her to marry him.

Three months after his father's death and the Marquis had not suggested a visit to Yorkshire, Cassandra was saying to herself:

"I cannot marry him."

She had been idealistic enough to believe romantically that when they met they would fall in love with each other and live happily ever afterwards.

She was well aware that she was beautiful and it would be unlikely for her not to appeal to the Marquis's taste in women.

Then she discovered grounds for thinking that he would in all respects be quite unresponsive to her attractions.

When she visited London the Spring before the *début* was cancelled because of the death of her grandfather, Cassandra had somewhat shyly asked her Aunt whether she would be likely to meet the Marquis of Charlbury at the Balls she would attend during the Season.

"The Marquis of Charlbury?" Lady

Fladbury had exclaimed, "Whatever makes you think that he might be a suitable partner?"

Her genuine surprise told Cassandra that the Duke and her father had kept their plans for their children a secret.

If there had been any gossip about their intentions, her Aunt quite certainly would have heard of it!

Cassandra did not answer and after a moment Lady Fladbury went on:

"But of course, I forgot, your father races with the Duke. Well, I should not bother your pretty head over young Charlbury. He is far too interested in the footlights to dance attendance on any debutante, however attractive!"

"In the footlights?" Cassandra questioned.

"He is one of the many 'men about town' who hang around the stage-door at the Gaiety," Lady Fladbury explained. "There are a whole number of them making fools of themselves over pretty girls who have no breeding and who most certainly will not make them good wives."

"Good wives?"

Cassandra was aware that actresses were considered fast and extremely improper and were not accepted by any society hostesses.

"Kate Vaughan, who starred at the Gaiety, married the Honourable Arthur Wellesley, nephew of the great Duke of Wellington, last year," Lady Fladbury said. "And Billie Bilton is now the Countess of Clancarty. The Earl has made an idiot of himself and his mother is in despair, as you can well imagine."

"I did not realise that gentlemen actually . . . married actresses," Cassandra said.

"These women are very astute!" her Aunt replied. "They make the men who pursue them so infatuated that they cannot escape from escorting them up the aisle!"

"And you are saying that the Marquis of Charlbury is also . . . interested in these . . . actresses?"

"They do not do much acting — not on the stage at any rate!" Lady Fladbury snapped. "But they are very gay, their faces are painted like a herbaceous border, and their jewels glitter as my old Nurse used to describe it, 'like the devil's eye-balls!' "

She laughed:

"Oh well, do not worry, my dear! There are plenty of other men in the world besides those who are dazzled by the glittering lights in the Strand."

She did not see the expression on her niece's face because Cassandra had turned away, astonished and shocked by what she had heard.

When she had the opportunity she talked to her father, knowing that Sir James would tell her the truth. She only half-believed the gossip which came so easily to her Aunt's lips.

"Aunt Eleanor says that many young men are actually marrying actresses from the Gaiety, Papa. Is not that somewhat . . . unusual?"

Sir James had glanced at her quickly before he replied:

"Certainly not as many as your Aunt makes out. The majority of the men, Cassandra, find it amusing to take actresses out to supper and give them presents."

He paused to continue as if he sought for words.

"A man disports himself in the company of these ladies with a freedom which would not be permitted by any Chaperon and certainly not by any jealous husband."

"Are they very . . . pretty?" Cassandra asked.

"Extremely!" Sir James replied. "And they are easygoing, which young men find attractive in contrast to the stiff formality of more respectable occasions."

He spoke lightly and then as if he realised

why Cassandra was questioning him, he said with a perception which surprised her:

"Have you been hearing stories about Varro Charlbury?"

Cassandra did not reply, and after a moment he said:

"I thought you might have. A young man, my dearest, has to sow his wild oats. In most cases he makes a better husband because of it."

"But . . . supposing he falls . . . in love?" Cassandra asked in a low voice.

"The word 'love'," he said after a moment, "reflects a multitude of emotions. What a man feels for an attractive woman of the type of whom we have just been speaking, is not really love, but desire."

He watched Cassandra's face, and went on:

"It gets dolled up in a great many pretty words, but he wants not only to be amused by these women, but also to feel free, untrammelled!"

He paused before he added:

"Unless a man is very stupid, he has no wish to spend the rest of his life with a lovely face that has nothing behind it."

"Aunt Eleanor was saying. . . ."

"Your Aunt is exaggerating a few isolated instances where men have married what are known as 'Gaiety Girls' thinking that what they were doing was worth the cost."

Sir James paused a moment before he went on:

"They pay a very high penalty for what you call 'falling in love'. A man who is in the Army must leave his Regiment. If he is in the Diplomatic Corps or in Politics, the same thing applies. His wife will not be accepted in most instances by his mother or by any of his relatives, and even if his menfriends visit him, their wives will refuse any invitation."

Cassandra gave a little sigh.

"It seems unfair."

"Society has to have rules, and the rules where a man marries a woman beneath his station, or one who is notorious because she is an actress or has been divorced, are very, very stringent."

Sir James looked at Cassandra's serious face and added:

"Do not worry over the tales you may hear about Charlbury. I am convinced it is all a passing phase, and when he marries he will settle down and be an extremely respectable and respected Duke."

But things had not quite worked out the way Sir James had expected.

When the new Duke of Alchester had not

suggested, after his father's death, that he should make his postponed visit to The Towers, Cassandra contrived in one way or another to make enquiries about him.

She had found, as she had anticipated, that he was incessantly in the company of the Gaiety Girls or of other actresses.

"Alchester is known as 'The Merry Marquis,'" one of Cassandra's hunting acquaintances told her. "Have you never met him?"

"No," Cassandra answered. "I was only interested because, as you know, Papa and the old Duke did a lot of racing together, and I was just wondering if the new holder of the title had kept up the stable."

"If he has, I expect he will soon have to sell up," her friend replied.

"Why?" Cassandra enquired.

"I believe he is badly dipped."

If this was so, Cassandra asked herself, why then did not the new Duke of Alchester fall back on the arrangements which had been made before his father's death and push ahead with the marriage which would bring him, through his wife, an enormous fortune?

She could find only one reasonable explanation.

It was that, despite everything her father might say, the Duke was in love and had no wish to make an arranged marriage.

By the time the winter of 1885 had come and there was no word from him, she was convinced that her father's plans had finally and completely gone astray and that they were unlikely to hear any more from the Duke.

But Sir James was optimistic.

"There could be no question of your being married while Alchester is in deep mourning," he said. "He will wait the conventional year. Then I am sure we shall take up the negotiations where they were left off."

'I will not be treated in such a manner!' Cassandra told herself, although she did not say the words aloud to her father.

Every month that passed strengthened her determination.

She would not marry a man whose heart was given elsewhere, and who wanted her for one reason and one reason only, that she was rich!

She saw now how childish her expectation had been that because she was pretty he would fall in love with her.

She might have far more brains and certainly be far more cultured than the women with whom he associated in London, but that was not to say that he would prefer such qualities.

She took to studying the photographs published of the actresses who were beguiling London audiences.

It was hard not to see that they certainly looked far more attractive and indeed more amusing than the stiff portraits of the society girls with whom they competed for the gentlemen's affections.

There were exceptions of course, if one compared them with the beautiful young Lady Warwick or the goddess-like Countess of Dudley.

'But who,' Cassandra asked herself, 'looks as attractive as Nelly Farran of whom the theatre critics say, "The Gaiety without Nelly is unthinkable," or Connie Gilchrist who has found fame with a skipping rope?'

Instead of cutting out from the newspapers pictures of the Duke of Alchester, Cassandra began to collect reproductions of the photographic beauties.

Photographs of them filled the shop-windows and were in many of the illustrated papers.

There had been loud criticism about one of the poses assumed by Maud Branscombe who was the first of the photographic beauties. She had figured in a study which portrayed 'the Rock of Ages'.

"Can you imagine that woman daring to

display herself clinging to the Cross?" Aunt Eleanor had asked. "I cannot think why the Bishops do not protest about it!"

There were a great many other lovely smiling actresses whose photographs could be bought for less than a shilling.

Cassandra had been amused when her father, protesting about the photographs that had been taken of her in York, produced from a locked drawer in his desk some pictures of Mrs. Langtry.

"This is the sort of pose that I want," he said.

He showed her a picture of 'the Jersey Lily' leaning gracefully on a high table, the shadow of her perfect features portrayed upon a plain wall behind her.

"She looks very lovely, Papa," Cassandra agreed.

Her father had shown her several other photographs and then he said:

"There is no need to mention to your mother that I keep these. It is just that I was trying to explain to you the way I want you to appear."

"I quite understand, Papa."

Sir James put the photographs away in his drawer.

"Photography may be a new art," he said, "but that is not going to stop every half-witted fool who can afford a camera thinking he is a photographer."

Turning over the pages of the album which now covered no less than fourteen years of the Marquis of Charlbury's life, Cassandra told herself the whole thing was hopeless.

How could she marry a man who was interested in her only because she owned a fortune?

Her father might talk of a *mariage de convenance*. He might say it was usual in society, but there were still a large number of people who married for love, and she wished to be one of them.

She had been thinking about it for a long time — in fact for all the months that her father had been eagerly awaiting a letter from the new Duke. She had felt certain it would not arrive.

She had been wrong!

But she was sure that it had eventually turned up, not because the Duke wanted to see her, but because he had reached the stage where he needed money too desperately to procrastinate any longer.

She stared at an article giving a long description of Alchester Park which had appeared in the *Illustrated London News*.

It was not hard from the description, to imagine the splendour of what was one of the most famous houses in England.

Covering several acres of land, the ancestral seat of the Dukes of Alchester, it had been built in the reign of Elizabeth I and had housed at some time or another, almost every reigning Monarch.

It was magnificent, it was splendid, a little overpowering, and yet Cassandra could understand it was a suitable back-ground for the young man of whom the newspapers had written such glowing accounts even when he was a mere boy.

She turned the pages of the Album again. His face looked out at her from every one.

He was not so thin and so sharp-featured as he had been when he captained the Eton Eleven, but his hair still grew back in a straight line from his forehead.

Even in the rather harsh photograph sketches which were the nearest the illustrated papers could get to reproducing photographs, his eyes still seemed to hold that curious searching look she had noticed when she first saw him.

She had loved her memories of him, she had loved every scrap of information she could glean about him. But now she realised she no longer wanted to marry him.

Cassandra gave a little sigh.

'I would rather marry a man for whom I had no feelings at all,' she told herself.

That was indeed true.

It might be unpleasant, even a little frightening, to marry someone she hardly knew and for whom she had no affection!

But to marry someone with whom she thought herself in love would be sheer unmitigating hell if he had no feeling for her except one of duty.

It would be his duty to touch her . . . it would be his duty to kiss her . . . It would be his duty to make love to her . . . to give her children . . .

Cassandra, like all her contemporaries, was very innocent and was not quite certain what that entailed. But she knew it must be something close and intimate.

"Mama, why do people who sleep in the same bed have babies?" she had asked Lady Alice once, when she was very young.

Lady Alice had hesitated before she replied:

"When you are married, Cassandra, your husband will explain such things to you."

Cassandra would have asked again, but sometimes she puzzled over it.

Now she knew she could not sleep in the same bed with a man she loved, as she loved the Marquis, but who did not love her.

"I could not bear it!" she said aloud.

She closed the Albums with a bang and put them back in the bottom drawer of her bureau.

Then she drew from the same secret drawer where she hid the key another book bound with leather, and started to write.

Ever since she had been quite young, Sir James had encouraged his daughter to keep a diary.

"You are growing up," he had said, "in a world of change — a world where everything will be very different from what we knew in the past. There are new inventions and new discoveries every day and new thoughts which should be recorded."

He smiled at Cassandra.

"You will also meet new people and have many contacts with those who are famous. Put it all down. If nothing else, you will have the history of your own life to read when you are old. I have always regretted more than I can possibly say that I never recorded mine."

Obediently, because she always did as her father wished her to do, Cassandra kept her diary.

She wrote in it every evening before she went to bed, until there were already a number of volumes locked away, while the current book was kept at hand in her secret drawer.

She showed it to no-one, not even to her father, although occasionally when something happened which she had anticipated she would read him extracts.

Then he would admire her perspicacity and the fact that what she had expected had occurred, almost exactly as she had predicted.

Cassandra wrote now for only a short time, then put the book back in the secret drawer and shut it. Moving from her Sitting-room she went into her bed-room.

As she walked across the thick carpet to the mirror over her Dressing-table, she stared at her own reflection but she was thinking of something very different.

"I must see him first," she said aloud. "I want to be sure that I am doing the right thing before I upset Papa."

As if her thoughts moved from her inward preoccupation to her visual appearance, she looked critically at herself.

Her red-gold hair loosened by Hannah had been brushed until every strand, shining vividly in the lights of the dressing-table, seemed to dance tempestuously over her head.

Her blue eyes in vivid contrast stared back at her from between their long dark lashes.

"It is most unfair!" one of Cassandra's

friends had exclaimed petulantly. "I spend hours trying to think how I can darken my eye-lashes without Mama being aware of it, and yours are as black as ink."

"They are quite natural, I assure you," Cassandra said laughingly.

"I am aware of that," her friend had replied. "That's just what makes it so unfair! If your white skin, your dark eye-lashes and your red hair owed their appearance to artifice, they would be easier to bear. As it is, Cassandra, you look deliciously, flamboyantly theatrical, without making any effort to do so."

Cassandra could hear the touch of envy in her friend's voice, but now she remembered the words.

"Flamboyantly theatrical!"

'It is true,' she thought and knew it was the same criticism which the older generation leveled against her.

"She is pretty, very pretty," she had heard one Dowager say disagreeably, "but far too theatrical for my taste!"

"Flamboyantly theatrical!"

Cassandra had often repeated the words to herself, and because she was given to telling herself stories and imagining situations which intrigued her just before she went to sleep, she had invented one in which she had become a Gaiety Girl.

Losing all her money, she had gone to London and approached George Edwards with a request that she might be in the chorus.

"You are too pretty for that, my dear," he would reply. "I will give you a part, and let us see if the audience will appreciate you as enthusiastically as the 'Stage-door Johnnies'."

Of course in Cassandra's imagination, she had been a success over-night.

She had been applauded until the Gaiety Theatre had shaken with the noise of it, and there had been a queue of ardent admirers in their top hats, white ties and tails waiting to take her out to supper.

And naturally in her dreams the one whom she had bestowed her favour was the Duke of Alchester.

'A child's imagination,' she had told herself during the last six months, when despite every resolution the dream had returned to her.

Why should she not compete with the Gaiety Girls? Why should they have all the fun and collect all the men? Or was she worrying about only one man in particular?

There were a million questions which presented themselves and to which she could find no answer.

Now she knew that in some subtle and insidious way her adolescent dreams had become so much a part of her thinking that they were assuming reality.

It was mad! It was crazy! It was a recklessness that would exceed anything she had ever done before, and yet she was determined to meet the Duke on his own ground.

She would see him as he was when he was not pretending, when he was not putting on an act for her father's benefit and for hers.

'I have to do it,' she told her own reflection in the mirror. 'I must do it! I cannot go on allowing Papa to live in a Fool's Paradise, thinking that I shall agree to his plans when I have no intention of doing so.'

She had been so sure ever since Christmas that the Duke would not write, and that sooner or later Sir James would have to realise that for once in his life he had lost a race.

It was just her father's proverbial luck, Cassandra thought, now that his horse should romp home at the last moment. It was the sort of thing that always happened to Sir James!

'But this time,' she told herself bitterly, 'there is going to be no gold cup for the winner.'

She walked across her bed-room restlessly, knowing it would be impossible for her to go to bed and sleep until everything was settled in her mind.

'Supposing,' her brain said to her, 'when you see the Duke you fall crazily in love with him — more in love than you have ever been?'

'I still will not marry him if he cares for someone else,' Cassandra answered.

Even as she spoke the words beneath her breath she wondered if they were true.

Would she be strong enough to refuse to marry the man she loved, to turn away from him, even if he was willing to marry her, because she could not endure the humiliation of loving where she was not loved?

"How could I be fool enough to think he would come to care for me in time?"

She knew she had more pride than that.

If she was convinced in her mind that he really loved someone else then she would be strong enough to say "No".

"I shall never be sure whether he is telling me the truth or not unless I see him when he is off his guard," Cassandra said to herself.

She had in fact thought this all out quite a long time ago, and whilst she dismissed it as sheer nonsense, she knew that like her father she was merely planning ahead.

All she had to do now was to translate her thoughts into action.

She would go to London. She had already decided that. And it was a genuine excuse for her to wish to buy clothes.

Somehow she must meet the Duke, not as Cassandra Sherburn, but as an actress, as the type of woman in whom he was interested.

She would be gay, amusing, sparkling with a *joie de vivre* which he could not find among simpering young girls or even the sophisticated society women who sought his company because he was the bearer of a noble title.

Almost like a puzzle, the pieces fell into place, making a complete picture that Cassandra could look at and know that, in its own way, it was faultless.

She had already told herself a long time ago that Lily Langtry would be a passport to the glittering world she was determined to enter.

To Cassandra her father's friendship with the Jersey Lily implied only a discreet flirtation. She had no awareness of physical passion, which had never intruded upon her sheltered life.

She thought she understood that her father, so handsome, so attractive to women and so masculine, must find it hard at times to be tied to her injured mother.

He would in consequence occasionally escape from the conventional role he played to perfection to enjoy himself in London, to take a pretty woman out to supper and dance with her, as her poor mother could never dance again.

Sir James's love affairs never encroached upon his home.

There were numerous women in the County who pursued him quite shamelessly. He flattered them and paid them compliments, but he made quite certain that as far as he was concerned that was the beginning and the end of their association.

It would have violated his principles to go any further.

In Yorkshire he was the devoted husband, a man of integrity and responsibility, who had built up an impregnable position of authority in the County and was respected by all who knew him.

What he did in London was in fact nobody's business.

On his periodic journeys which involved attending race meetings and Tattersalls Sales, buying pictures and furniture, there were evenings when Sir James was certainly not dining in Park Lane with his Stepsister.

Nor was he at the Banquets, Dinner Parties or the Royal occasions graced by the Prince of Wales, to which he was invited.

If on his return home there was a flood of tinted envelopes, jauntily perfumed, and impetuous telegrams, neither Lady Alice nor Cassandra was aware of them.

But sometimes when her father was away, Cassandra thought her mother seemed a little more restless, and very occasionally she would protest against the fate which kept her tied to a wheel-chair.

At other times Lady Alice never complained. Never in front of her husband by word or deed did she ever draw attention to her helplessness or invite his sympathy.

Instead she made herself so attractive that when people stayed in the house or were entertained at The Towers, they would often say to Cassandra afterwards:

"You know, I keep forgetting that your mother is confined to a wheel-chair. She is so unbelievably brave and never makes anyone embarrassed by referring to it that I always think of her as living quite a normal life."

"My father and I feel like that too," Cassandra would reply, and it had in fact been the truth.

But there was no disguising the unutterable gladness on Lady Alice's face when Sir

James returned from London!

Her arms would go out to him with a cry of welcome which to Cassandra was more moving and revealing than any words.

"Have you missed me, my darling?" Cassandra heard her father say once as he bent to put his arms around his wife.

"You know that every moment when we are apart seems like an eternity of emptiness," Lady Alice replied.

Cassandra had felt the tears come into her eyes as she recognized the throb of anguish in her mother's voice.

'That is love!' she told herself now. 'Love is when one can sacrifice one's own feelings so that the other person shall be happy! At the same time, Mama knows that Papa loves her with all his heart.'

It would be different where she and the Duke were concerned: he would have no love for her, only a sense of duty.

"I cannot bear it! I cannot bear it!" she said aloud again.

She decided that if her plan failed, if she learnt that the Duke's heart belonged elsewhere, then she would brave her father's anger and would refuse categorically to marry him, whatever the consequences.

Cassandra took off her silk wrapper and got into bed.

"I will give him a fair chance," she said aloud. "In fact he shall have more than a chance. I am giving myself a handicap in my efforts to be sporting about it!"

She tried to smile at the racing jargon but failed.

Instead she buried her face in the pillow and tried to think, not of the Duke of Alchester, but the part she must play in attempting to deceive him.

In the train to London Cassandra went over her plans a dozen times, and it seemed as if the wheels of the train sounded an accompaniment to what she was thinking.

'It is crazy — it is crazy — it is crazy!' the wheels were saying.

Cassandra had known it was crazy when she awoke in the morning and having dressed, had gone first to her mother to receive last minute instructions about taking good care of herself.

"Buy the loveliest gowns you can find, darling," her mother said. "I am sure Bond Street will be full of delectable confections!"

"I will certainly try to find some dresses you will like," Cassandra answered.

"But come back as soon as you can," Lady Alice admonished.

"I promise I will do that," Cassandra answered. "A little of Aunt Eleanor's gossip goes a very long way!"

Lady Alice laughed.

"I should not tell her the Duke is coming to stay. You know she can never keep a secret."

"I never tell Aunt Eleanor anything that I do not wish to be known all around Mayfair within the next half an hour," Cassandra laughed.

On the door-step she put her arms around her father's neck.

"I wish you were coming with me, Papa," she said. "But you know if you did I should never get anything done. Without you I shall concentrate on spending a large amount of your money."

"You have only to write a cheque on Coutts Bank and they will let you have everything you require," Sir James said. "You have enough with you now?"

"More than enough."

Cassandra kissed him again and got into the closed carriage where Hannah was already seated, stiff and still somewhat disagreeable about having to pack in such a hurry.

The horses set off and Cassandra waved to her father until a turn of the drive took them out of sight of the house.

Then she leaned back in the carriage.

"Hannah," she said, "we are off on a great adventure."

The maid looked at her suspiciously.

"What do you mean by that, Miss Cassandra?"

"You are going to help me to do something quite outrageous," Cassandra answered.

"I'm going to do nothing of the sort," Hannah said stiffly. "If you're up to any of your tricks, Miss Cassandra, I'm going back to Her Ladyship at this very moment."

Cassandra laughed.

"Oh, Hannah, I love to tease you! You always rise to any bait I cast under your nose. What I am going to do will not be too shocking, but I need your help."

"I'm not doing anything of which Her Ladyship would not approve," Hannah said stoutly.

But Cassandra knew that she could rely on her to help her as she had always done in other escapades however reprehensible.

It was a long, rather tiring journey to London, but Cassandra did not notice either the landscape speeding past them or that the hours seemed long drawn out.

She was planning, scheming, working out every detail of what she intended to do.

Her father had often said it was a pity she had not been a boy, and because he had no son, he used to talk to her of his business schemes and developments.

He often tried out on her new ideas before he put them to a Board of Directors, or sounded her to find out whether a new approach to a difficult problem would get the response he intended.

Cassandra learned from him the importance of every tiny detail, when something new was to be put into operation.

"It is always the weakest link in the chain which can prove disastrous," was one of her father's favorite remarks.

Cassandra knew now that in her present scheming, the weakest link in the chain would be the risk of exposure.

Hannah thought she was very quiet but said nothing. She did however look anxiously at her young mistress. She had been used to her chatter and was finding this serious mood almost frightening.

But Cassandra was smiling when finally they arrived at Sir James's house in Park Lane, where the bow windows on the ground and first floors overlooked the green trees of Hyde Park.

The residence was the acme of comfort, Sir James having even installed the new incandescent electric light which was the last word in sensational novelty and a telephone. The first Exchange having been opened in London in 1879.

Lady Fladbury had in her youth been a pretty girl. She had however grown stout and heavy in her old age, and at sixty found it impossible to move quickly.

She was ten years older than her Stepbrother but was devoted to him, and she had a real affection for Cassandra.

"I had been wondering when you would visit me again," she said when her niece appeared, "and I cannot tell you how delighted I was when I received your father's telegram this morning."

"It is delightful to see you, Aunt Eleanor. I have come to London to buy some new clothes. I have also a number of social engagements, so I shall not be a trouble to you."

"You are never that," Lady Fladbury replied. "At the same time, I was wondering if I should cancel the Bridge party I have arranged for tomorrow night."

"No, please," Cassandra begged, "do not cancel anything, Aunt Eleanor. I am practically booked up the whole of the time I am here. In fact I was half-afraid you might feel offended that I can spend so little time with you."

"No, of course not. All I want is for you to

enjoy yourself," her Aunt replied.

Cassandra sipped the hot chocolate which the butler had set down by her side.

"Tell me all the gossip, Aunt Eleanor," she begged. "You know as well as I do that living in the wilds of Yorkshire we never hear any scandal until it is out of date."

Lady Fladbury laughed.

"I cannot believe that," she said, "but there are quite a lot of amusing incidents which are the *on dit* of the moment."

She chattered away about a number of their acquaintances.

"To whom is the Prince of Wales attached now?" Cassandra asked.

"Far too many lovely women for me to enumerate," Lady Fladbury replied. "But one thing is very certain; since Mrs. Langtry, His Royal Highness's lady friends, even if they are actresses, are accepted in some sections of society."

Cassandra laughed.

"A crown can work marvels! But I see no reason why an actress should be treated as a pariah!"

Lady Fladbury appeared to be about to reply. Then changed what she was about to say to a question.

"What about you, Cassandra. Have you not any plans to marry?"

"Not yet," Cassandra answered. "I have yet to find someone who will capture my heart."

"It surprises me that James has no-one in mind for you," her Aunt said reflectively. "He always used to talk when you were a child as if he expected you to marry at least a Prince, and yet here you are over twenty and still a spinster."

"But not quite an old maid," Cassandra protested.

"I was wondering the other day who would suit you," Lady Fladbury remarked, "and I have quite a long list of eligible young men who would welcome a pretty, intelligent and of course wealthy young wife."

As Cassandra made no comment, she continued:

"I thought your father would be certain to bring you to London for the Season. He has not asked me to apply to Buckingham Palace that I might present you, so I assume he has done so himself."

"I expect so," Cassandra said indifferently. "The last Drawing-room does not take place until the end of May. That gives us plenty of time."

"If you are to be presented, your father surely would have told you so."

"Perhaps he had not received an answer,"

Cassandra replied. "I feel I am too old to be a debutante."

"Nonsense!" Lady Fladbury exclaimed. "You will have to be presented sooner or later. It looks as if it will have to be on your marriage."

"When I find a husband!"

Cassandra hesitated a moment and then she said:

"Perhaps, as you told me some time ago, all the eligible bachelors have been caught by the Gaiety Girls. Are there any more heart throbs among the aristocracy?"

"Quite a number," Lady Fladbury replied. "There is a joke going around that the Duke of Beaufort, who is a Knight of the Garter, was asked by an inquisitive Frenchman what the letters 'K.G.' stood for after his name, and he answered 'Konnie Gilchrist'."

Cassandra laughed.

"Are there many noblemen among the Stage-door Johnnies?"

"Too many of them for me to tell you about them all," her Aunt replied.

Cassandra took a deep breath. She realised she would have to risk being more direct to elicit the information she really wanted.

"What about the son of Papa's great racing friend, the Duke of Alchester?" She tried to make her voice sound casual. "Is the young Duke's name connected with anyone in particular?"

"During the Winter he was always with an actress," her Aunt replied. "I cannot remember her name. Betty somebody. But I do not think it was serious. Nevertheless there is no doubt he has a passion for Gaiety Girls. Lady Lowry was saying only last week that he refuses all invitations to any of the respectable parties."

"Do you think he will marry someone on the stage?" Cassandra asked.

"I should not be surprised," her Aunt answered. "Lady Lowry tells us that the men who are infatuated with these painted creatures are too stage-struck to be quite sane!"

"Perhaps that is the . . . explanation," Cassandra murmured despondently.

Chapter Three

Cassandra woke early the following morning and, realising she had an hour before Hannah would come and call her, she rose to draw back the curtains in her bedroom.

She then took from the drawer in which she had placed it the night before the letter her father had given her addressed to Mrs. Langtry.

She looked at the envelope, then deliberately opened it.

Sir James had written in his strong, upright, hand-writing:

"Most Exquisite Lily,

I am so thrilled, as are all those who love you, by the huge success you have achieved on both sides of the Atlantic. I saw you in 'Peril' and thought you were not only brilliant but looking if possible, more beautiful than ever.

This is to introduce my daughter, of whom I am very proud. Like so many other people she is longing to meet the most lovely woman in the world. I know you will be sweet to her, Lily, and

I am grateful, as I have always been grateful to you for your kindness.

At your feet — as ever,

My love,
James."

Cassandra read it through carefully. She thought it was very gushing, but she supposed that someone like Mrs. Langtry would expect a man to be effusive.

Taking a sheet of engraved paper which she had brought with her from The Towers, she started to copy her father's handwriting.

She had done it before to amuse herself.

"You write so much better than anyone I have ever known, Papa," she had said. "At the same time your writing is so clear and distinctive it would be easy for a forger to defraud you."

"Perhaps he would not be as skilful as you," Sir James had laughed, "but anyway I will be careful that you do not bankrupt me!"

Now Cassandra found that after a few efforts it would have been impossible for anyone who was not an expert to detect that the letter she had written had not been inscribed by Sir James himself.

Then, where he had started: "This is to

introduce . . ." she copied exactly the first part of his letter and she wrote instead:

"This is to introduce Miss Sandra Standish a young actress who is the daughter of an old friend, and to ask you if, with your usual generosity, you would grant her a quite simple request. You are someone whom she worships from afar, but apart from the great honour of meeting you she is very anxious for an introduction to the young Duke of Alchester.

"It is something as you know, I could easily do myself but unfortunately I cannot for the moment find time to visit London. So please, dearest Lily, help Miss Standish and when we next meet I shall once again be in your debt."

Cassandra finished the letter as her father had done and re-wrote the envelope. She tore into small pieces her father's letter and several mistakes she had made in her first efforts at copying it.

Rising to her feet she put the letter away. Then an idea struck her.

She crossed the room to the dressing-table and took from the bottom drawer the jewel case with which she always traveled and which Hannah never let out of her hand.

It held a great deal of jewellery for someone so young, but Sir James liked his women to glitter, and both Cassandra and her mother received at Christmas and on their birthdays fabulous gems.

From the bottom of the case, Cassandra drew out a leather box which contained, reposing on a velvet lining, a large diamond star.

It was one of the few presents her father had given her which she had thought did not measure up to his usual exquisite taste. There was something a little garish and ornate about it.

The diamonds were too large and the setting not as delicate as the presents he usually chose, but she was aware that it was a valuable piece.

She thought as she looked at it that it would be a very suitable present for someone like Mrs. Langtry.

Cassandra had been surprised at the number and value of Mrs. Langtry's jewels, of which the papers gave long and elaborate descriptions every time she appeared.

The story of her climb to fame when she had appeared in London with her husband, so poor that she had only one black dress, had been reiterated over and over again.

Just as the Prince of Wales's infatuation had lost nothing in the telling, even to those who lived as far away as Yorkshire.

What was inexplicable was the thousands of pounds worth of jewels Mrs. Langtry suddenly acquired, despite the fact that she was so poor she had to earn money by going on the stage.

'But of course, since she is so beautiful, people want to give her presents,' Cassandra told herself and the explanation seemed simple.

Cassandra thought it likely, because he rather enjoyed giving presents, that her father had contributed to the diamonds which had astounded America and even in England were referred to constantly in every newspaper.

She shut the box which contained the star, set it down on the writing table, and closing her own jewel-case replaced it in the drawer.

She opened the letter which she had already sealed and added a postscript:

"To me you have always been the most glittering star in the Universe."

Once again Cassandra wrote the envelope

and put the letter and the jewel box in a drawer of the writing-table which she locked.

When Hannah came to call her mistress she found her already half-dressed.

"Why didn't you ring the bell, Miss Cassandra?" Hannah enquired.

"I thought you might be having your breakfast," Cassandra answered, "and I did not wish to disturb you because we are going out as soon as you can be ready."

"At this hour of the morning?" Hannah asked in surprise.

"I have a lot to do," Cassandra answered. "I am sure, Hannah, you do not wish to stay in London any longer than is necessary."

She knew this was the best way of getting Hannah to do what she wanted because the maid hated Sir James's town house and always longed to be back at The Towers.

It was however two hours later before Cassandra had managed to have her breakfast and leave her Aunt without appearing rude.

Lady Fladbury had a whole repertoire of gossip to relate about friends, and an endless flow of tittle-tattle about the Socialites who filled the newspapers; so that Cassandra could hardly get a word in.

She wished to pick her Aunt's brains without appearing to do so, and finally she managed to say:

"I would like to visit the theatre whilst I am in London. What is Mrs. Langtry's new play like?"

"Rather amusing!" Lady Fladbury replied. "It is a comedy-drama called 'Enemies'. Another of Coghlan's adaptations from the French."

"Is it exciting?" Cassandra enquired.

"The second act concludes with murder by strangulation of a country girl in a fit of passion by a deaf and dumb idiot," Lady Fladbury answered, "if that makes you laugh!"

Cassandra smiled as her Aunt went on:

"I have to admit that Mrs. Langtry acted quite well. Of course she was extremely refined and ladylike — that goes without saying — but everyone says it is the best part she has played."

"I would like to see it," Cassandra said.

"Of course the Prince of Wales was at the opening night," Lady Fladbury continued, hardly pausing for breath.

"I expect Mrs. Langtry's clothes are very beautiful," Cassandra hazarded.

"Of course!" Lady Fladbury answered. "Since she does not pay for them, she can naturally afford the best."

"I suppose the theatre management think the expense a good advertisement," Cassandra remarked. "But where does she buy them?"

"Most of her clothes come from Worth or Doucet in Paris, but Redfern of Conduit Street, where the Princess of Wales shops, makes some of them."

"I have often been to Redfern," Cassandra murmured, but her Aunt was not listening.

"Have you heard the story that Alfred de Rothschild said he would give her a dress from Doucet, and Mrs. Langtry ordered an extra petticoat with it. When the bill came he sent it on to her, saying he had offered her one dress but no more."

Cassandra laughed. She did not like to show her ignorance by revealing that she thought it very strange that Mrs. Langtry should allow a man to give her a gown.

"She must be the envy of every other leading lady," she remarked. "Where do they purchase their gowns?"

"In ordinary and much cheaper shops," Lady Fladbury replied, "and you may be quite sure they resent it. At the same time, I am told, that Chasemore has done a wonderful job for George Edwardes at the Gaiety. I have not seen the new show, but it caused a lot of comment that he gave them the chance to dress his new production."

Cassandra had found out what she wished to know.

"I must go, Aunt Eleanor," she said. "I am keeping the horses waiting, and you know how much Papa dislikes my doing that!"

It was an excuse to which there was no reply, and Cassandra got away while she could to find Hannah waiting for her in the hall.

Cassandra gave the footman an address and they set off down Piccadilly.

It was a cold, blustery day, and she was glad of the warmth from her fur-trimmed jacket.

"Where are we going, Miss Cassandra?" Hannah enquired.

"Shopping," Cassandra answered, "and do not be surprised, Hannah, at anything I buy. This is the beginning of the adventure about which I warned you."

In spite of the warning, however, Hannah was extremely surprised and said so in no uncertain terms, when during the morning Cassandra purchased clothes of which the maid told her a dozen times her mother would not approve.

"You must have gone out of your mind, Miss Cassandra!" she said in horrified tones when the *Vendeuse* had left the Dressing-room to fetch a seamstress to alter one of the gowns.

There was no doubt the dress Cassandra was trying on was very different from the beautiful gowns she had previously worn.

They had been elaborate and many of them had had a decided Parisian chic about them. But what she was wearing now was glitteringly spectacular and accentuated her flamboyant red hair and dark-fringed eyes. It was also very theatrical.

"For goodness sake, Miss Cassandra, why are you wasting your money on this trash?" Hannah asked.

"I have my reasons," Cassandra answered enigmatically. "What do I look like, Hannah? Tell me the truth!"

"You look like something off the Music Hall, and what your father would say about you dolled up like some fast hussy from behind the footlights, I don't know."

"Thank you, Hannah, that is exactly what I wanted to hear," Cassandra answered.

She paid no attention to Hannah's protests and went on ordering, to the delight of the saleswoman.

"We made some really attractive gowns for Miss Sylvia Grey," the woman volunteered.

"She is in 'Little Jack Shepherd' at the Gaiety," Cassandra remarked.

"Yes, and one of her gowns, not unlike

the one you have on, Madam, was written up in several of the newspapers. But it is Miss Nelly Farran who gets the applause. She really pays for dressing, and she herself said she had never worn clothes which made her look better."

The woman recommended a milliner who had provided the bonnets for the leading ladies of 'Little Jack Shepherd', and Cassandra bought shoes and handbags to match each outfit.

Finally Hannah announced it was long after her luncheon time.

"And you'll be fainting on my hands if you don't have something to eat soon, Miss Cassandra," she said sharply. "Come along, now. You've wasted enough money and a real waste it is too! I can't see you wearing one of those vulgar garments, and that's a fact."

"You will be surprised, Hannah!" Cassandra answered.

She took one of the gowns and an evening wrap with her, and arranged for her other purchases to be delivered if not that evening, first thing the following morning.

Then she stopped the carriage at a shop called Clarksons.

Hannah looked up in disgust and exclaimed:

"Theatrical Wig-makers! You're never going to buy a wig, Miss Cassandra! If you do, I'll go straight back to Yorkshire and you'll not stop me."

"No, I want something quite different," Cassandra answered, "and you need not come in with me, Hannah. I can manage quite well by myself."

She went into the shop and found just inside the door there was a counter on which were displayed the grease-paint, lip-salves, powders and paints which were required by actors and actresses.

Such things were not obtainable in any of the shops she usually patronised.

She made several purchases and went back to the carriage.

"I want to know what's going on!" Hannah said. "If you want my help, Miss Cassandra, you'll have to tell me the truth."

Cassandra was as yet unwilling to reveal her secret plans even to Hannah.

She fobbed the maid off with excuses until finally they arrived back at Park Lane.

Lady Fladbury was not particularly interested in what her niece had been doing during the morning.

She had more bits of gossip she wished to relate to Cassandra, and she chattered away all through luncheon hardly giving her time to reply.

"Are you never bored, Aunt Eleanor, living here alone most of the time?"

Cassandra could not help thinking that Lady Fladbury must be lonely — otherwise she would not be so vivaciously voluble when she had an audience.

"I have never been happier in my life!" her Aunt replied with all sincerity. "The truth is, Cassandra, I have never in the past had a moment to think about myself. My husband was a very demanding man, and my children, before they grew up and married, were always expecting me to do what they wanted — never what I wanted to do myself."

She laughed.

"It is the lot of all women! Sometimes I remember that someone once said: — 'The best thing in life is to be born a widow and an orphan'. I think they were right!"

She smiled and added:

"Of course they meant a wealthy widow and orphan!"

"So you are now in that position," Cassandra remarked.

"I am not wealthy but, thanks to your father, I am comfortable. I have a great many friends in London and as long as I can sit down at a Bridge table, then there is no more contented woman than I am."

"I am so glad, Aunt Eleanor."

"I suppose if I were a good Chaperon," Lady Fladbury went on. "I should be making enquiries as to why you are so busy, but I am not going to ask any questions."

"Thank you, Aunt Eleanor," Cassandra smiled.

"All I ask is that you do not get me into trouble with your father."

"What the eye does not see, the heart does not grieve over," Cassandra quoted.

Then she rose from the Dining-room table and kissed her Aunt.

"You have always been very kind to me, Aunt Eleanor, and I am grateful."

"You are up to something, I know that!" Lady Fladbury laughed. "Run along with you! Everyone likes to keep their own secrets. I have three friends waiting for me at a green-baize table who will keep me occupied until it is dinner time."

To Hannah's mystification, Cassandra drove not to the shops but to a House-Agent's just off St. James's Street.

"What are we stopping here for?" the maid enquired.

"You wait in the carriage," Cassandra

said and disappeared before Hannah could say any more.

An Agent in a smart frock-coat was suitably impressed by Cassandra's appearance and her expensive fur-trimmed jacket.

"I am looking for a flat or apartment for a friend of mine," she explained. "She is on the stage."

"On the stage, Madam?" the Agent exclaimed in astonishment.

Cassandra knew that he thought it almost inconceivable that someone who looked like her should be connected with a woman in such a disreputable profession.

"She is a leading lady," Cassandra explained sweetly, "and the same type of person as Mrs. Langtry. She therefore wants to live somewhere in the West End so that she will be near the theatre, but it must not be, you understand, in a building with a bad reputation."

"No, of course not!" the Estate Agent said in shocked tones. "But you'll appreciate, Madam, it is not every landlord who'll accept actors and actresses."

"Presumably because they do not always pay their bills," Cassandra said with a little smile. "But let me set your mind at rest. My friend has asked me to put down two months rent in advance. That should annul any landlord's fears that financially he might be out of pocket."

"Yes, yes of course," the Agent agreed. "It'll make things very much easier."

He opened a large Ledger and looked through it with a little frown on his forehead.

Cassandra was quite certain that he was feeling embarrassed because he had so little to offer.

"You will understand," he said after a moment, "that we do not as a rule keep on our books the type of flat or lodgings which are patronised by your friend's profession."

"I understand," Cassandra said quietly, "but I remember hearing that at one time Mrs. Langtry had a flat in the Albany. Is there nothing available there?"

"I'm afraid not," the Agent replied, "but there's a flat in Bury Street. I don't know whether it would be suitable. The first floor flat was at one time occupied by Miss Kate Vaughan before she married."

"At least she is respectable now!" Cassandra exclaimed. "Her husband, I understand, is the nephew of the Duke of Wellington."

"Yes, Madam," the Agent answered, "and even when she was on the stage, Miss Vaughan would have been acceptable to most landlords."

"I am glad to hear that," Cassandra said. "I would not like my friend to feel uncomfortable when she comes to London or believe that she is unwelcome."

"I'm sure we will find her something which she'll like," the Agent said. "What about this flat in Bury Street?"

"You have the particulars?"

He consulted his Ledger.

"It has two bed-rooms, a sitting-room and a small kitchen."

"That sounds as if it would do," Cassandra said.

"It also was occupied at one time by someone of importance in the theatrical world," the Agent revealed. "And so the furnishings should be to your friend's taste."

"I should like to see the flat," Cassandra replied.

She and Hannah drove in the carriage to Bury Street while the Agent hurried after them on foot.

It was only a short distance and Cassandra stared up at the high building. Then having instructed Hannah to say nothing in front of the man, they climbed the staircase to the second floor.

Panting a little because he had been obliged to run in an effort to keep up with the horses, the Agent opened the door and ushered them into the flat.

It was with difficulty that Cassandra prevented herself from laughing.

It was in fact more gaudy and more theatrical than she could possibly have imagined.

The furniture was quite substantial but in poor taste. The sofas and chairs were upholstered in a vivid blue brocade and heaped with frilly pink cushions — most of them embroidered with beads or coloured silks.

Pictures of every sort and description smothered the walls, many of them cheap oleographs of Rome and Italy.

There were some photographs of actresses and a few actors. There were half a dozen framed posters and as they all starred a certain well known Music-Hall personality, it was not difficult to guess the name of the flat's previous occupant.

"Where is the owner?" Cassandra asked the Estate Agent.

"As a matter of fact, Madam, she is in Australia," he replied. "She is on tour, it is her — friend —" he coughed apologetically, "who has asked me to find a tenant while she is away."

The bed-room was even more fantastic than the Sitting-room.

Here the curtains were of sugar-pink, and

held up at the corners of the pelmets with over-gilt angels.

The brass bed-stead was draped with material of the same colour, hanging from a half-tester decorated with artificial flowers.

There were bows, frills, fringes and tassels everywhere one looked, and the walls were almost completely covered with mirrors.

"The owner must be very fond of her own face," Cassandra remarked innocently.

She did not see the glint of amusement in the Agent's eyes.

"I will take the flat," Cassandra went on and tried not to laugh at Hannah's horrified and disgusted expression.

She paid two months rent in advance as she had promised, and giving her friend's name as "Miss Standish" she took possession of the key.

A porter informed her that his wife would be willing to clean the flat on an hourly basis.

"Her has to stay longer, Ma'am, if the place is in a mess," he said frankly.

"I understand," Cassandra replied, "and my friend will be quite willing to pay by the hour."

"Will your friend, Madam, be moving in immediately?" the Agent asked.

"She should be arriving from the North this evening," Cassandra replied, "but if not, she will certainly be here tomorrow. I am so grateful to you for finding her somewhere to stay. She has a great dislike of hotels."

"I quite understand that," the Agent said sympathetically.

He was delighted at having got the flat off his hands. He would never have sunk to putting anything so garish on his books, if the 'friend' of the lady who had lived there had not been of social importance.

Cassandra bade him good-bye and then drove back towards Park Lane listening to a storm of protest from Hannah's lips.

"Now what's all this about, Miss Cassandra? I've never seen such a horrible place! It's not fit for someone like yourself even to enter, let alone to be living in!"

"It is for my theatrical friend," Cassandra answered.

"And who might she be?" Hannah asked. "You've never had any friends who are on the stage to my knowledge, and anyway the Master wouldn't allow it. You know that as well as I do."

"Her name is Sandra Standish," Cassandra answered.

"Sandra?" Hannah said suspiciously.

"That's what the Master sometimes calls you."

"Yes, I know," Cassandra answered, "and that is why I have used it for my second self. It is difficult to answer to a Christian name you do not remember."

"What are you trying to tell me?" Hannah enquired sternly.

"That I am going to act a part," Cassandra answered. "Do not look so shocked, Hannah, I am not going on the stage. I shall play the part of a young and talented actress."

"An actress!" Hannah exclaimed in tones of horror.

"I only hope I am good enough to get away with it," Cassandra said.

"The only thing you'll get yourself into is a lot of trouble," Hannah said menacingly. "You're not going to stay in that ghastly place?"

"No, but I have to have an address," Cassandra answered, "and you are going to wait there for me, Hannah, in the evening. This is, if anyone takes me out."

"I don't know what's going on," Hannah said angrily. "All I know, Miss Cassandra, is that you're buying yourself a heap of trouble and no good will come of it, you mark my words!"

"I am marking them," Cassandra assured her.

At the same time she prayed that Hannah was wrong and that her plan would not fail.

The Stage-door keeper of the Prince's Theatre looked up in surprise when, at 7:30 P.M. a lady dressed in what seemed to him to be the height of fashion appeared at the glass window behind which he habitually sat.

"What d'you want?" he asked suspiciously.

He was an old man who had been at the Prince's for over twenty-five years and was known amongst the cast as "Old Growler."

"I would like to see Mrs. Langtry."

"Well, you can't," he answered. "She sees no-one until after the performance, and then not many of 'em can get in."

"I am sure she is very popular," the lady replied, "and that is why I wish to see her now."

"I told you. She don't see no one at this time."

Cassandra put the letter down in front of him and laid on top of it a sovereign.

"Will you tell Mrs. Langtry that I have something very valuable to give her," she said, "and I cannot entrust it to anyone else, not even you."

'Old Growler' stared at the sovereign. There was a greedy look in his eyes.

He was used to tips from the top-hatted gentlemen who called after the performance, but it was not often the feminine sex were so generous.

"I'll see what I can do," he said at length grudgingly and pocketed the sovereign with a swiftness which came from long practice.

He picked up the note and Cassandra heard his footsteps echoing on the flagged floor as he went along a narrow passage and disappeared up a winding iron staircase.

She waited thinking that this was the first time she had ever been backstage and realised how unattractive it was. The walls have been written on in pencil and it must have been years since they had been painted.

There was the smell of dirt, dust and grease-paint and it was also extremely cold. Cassandra pulled her velvet wrap closer around her shoulders.

She wished she could have worn one of her furs, but she felt it would have seemed too extravagant for someone who was not a name in the theatre world.

She waited impatiently.

Supposing after all Mrs. Langtry would not see her? She felt quite certain that what she had said about having something valuable to give her would have been repeated by the door-keeper and would have made the lady curious.

After all, Sir James would undoubtedly have been very generous in the past. He always was.

She heard the footsteps of the door-keeper returning long before she saw him and finally he appeared to say gruffly:

"Come this way."

Cassandra, with a little throb of her heart, followed him down the passage.

The place seemed to get even dirtier as she progressed, but when they entered Mrs. Langtry's brilliantly lit Dressing-room, it was to find it exactly as she had expected it would be.

She had read in one of the newspapers: —

"Mrs. Langtry insists on having each Dressing-room, in whatever theatre she is appearing, arranged as to furniture, etc., as nearly as alike as possible. This is one of the first things her Stage-manager attends to on reaching a City. Most of the paraphernalia is carried with her when Mrs. Langtry is on tour."

The Dressing-room, Cassandra saw, was not large and the most important piece of furniture was the dressing-table which was of white wood heavily enameled in white.

It was elaborately ornamented with cupids and butterflies and festooned with old rose satin lined with muslin.

The mirror was electro-lighted and there was a tray on the table containing Mrs. Langtry's toilet set. The brush, comb, scent bottle and powder-box were of gold, each engraved with her initials, the monograms being surrounded by a ring of turquoises.

Cassandra only had a quick look at the dressing-table before she saw there were baskets of flowers all round the walls and a cosy sofa decked with cushions of every sort of design.

Then from behind a high painted screen which was piled across a corner of the room Mrs. Langtry appeared, wearing a blue silk negligee.

Cassandra had expected her to be beautiful, but her photographs and pictures certainly did not do her justice.

At thirty-three Lily Langtry was breathtaking.

Her little Greek head and Greek features were so perfectly proportioned as to make one feel that one looked at an exquisite statue.

Her skin was transparent, so white and

delicate that one could only stare and believe that every other woman must have a quite different covering to her bones.

As Mrs. Langtry moved towards Cassandra with her hand outstretched she remembered that when he painted her, Sir John Millais had said:

"To see Lily Langtry walk is as though you saw a beautiful hound set upon its feet."

"How kind of you to bring me a letter from Sir James Sherburn," Mrs. Langtry said and her voice was low, soft and musical.

She smiled at Cassandra and walking to the sofa, settled herself comfortably against the cushions and patted the place beside her.

"Come and sit down, Miss Standish," she said. "You must tell me about yourself, but first I believe you have something for me."

Cassandra held out the jewel box which she had wrapped in tissue paper.

"Sir James said I was to give this into your hands, Mrs. Langtry, and entrust it to no-one else."

It seemed to her as if Mrs. Langtry took the box almost eagerly and, pulling off the tissue paper, opened it.

The large star glittered in the lights from the dressing-table.

"It is charming!" she said and Cassandra felt the words were almost a purr of appreciation.

She took the broach out of the box, examined it and replaced it on its velvet bed.

"And now," she said with a smile. "I understand you wish me to do something for you. Are you acting in London at the moment?"

"No, I have come South to have singing lessons," Cassandra answered. "I have been promised a part in a Musical play if I improve my voice, and so I intend to spend a month in London just working with a teacher."

"That's very sensible," Mrs. Langtry approved. "And while you are here you are anxious to meet the young Duke of Alchester?"

"I should be very grateful if you could introduce me to him," Cassandra said.

Mrs. Langtry raised her eyebrows and Cassandra saw the curiosity in her eyes.

"Varro is a friend of mine," she said. "Do tell me why you are so anxious to meet him?"

Cassandra dropped her voice.

"I have a message for him from someone who is now . . . dead."

"Then your meeting can be quite easily

arranged," Mrs. Langtry assured her. "As a matter of fact, I am going to a party this evening where it is almost certain he will be present. It is being given by Lord Carwen and he will not mind in the least if I take you with me. This is, if you have no other engagement?"

"No, none," Cassandra replied, "although I was hoping to see you act."

"Then that of course is something you must do. I have a friend who always sits in the stage-box. You shall watch the play with him and afterwards we will take you with us to Lord Carwen's party."

"How kind . . . how very kind you are," Cassandra said in heart-felt tones.

She noticed that while Mrs. Langtry was speaking her eyes had flickered over her evening-dress and noted that not only was it new and expensive but also the diamond brooch she wore pinned to the bodice was real as was the bracelet she wore over her kid gloves.

She could not help feeling that Mrs. Langtry might not have been so kind had she in fact been an impoverished, badly dressed young actress.

Nevertheless, Mrs. Langtry gave another glance at the star-brooch, doubtless appreciating the largeness of the diamonds, before she walked across to her dressing-table to place it in a drawer.

"Have you not to change?" Cassandra asked. "Would you like me to wait in the theatre?"

"No, you cannot go there alone," Mrs. Langtry said. "You must wait for Mr. Gebhard to arrive, and then he will take you to the Box. In the meantime, sit in that chair in the corner and keep very quiet. I have about fifteen minutes to rest before my dresser will begin to get me ready."

The next three-quarters of an hour was to Cassandra one of the most interesting experiences she had ever had.

When Mrs. Langtry rose from the couch where she had lain with closed eyes, her hair-dresser had arrived to arrange her hair, and the dresser to get her elaborate gowns ready for the performance.

Cassandra saw that the mirror was electro-lighted to Mrs. Langtry's own special design, and an ingenious arrangement of colours such as blue, red and amber could be obtained at will.

"This makes it easy," Mrs. Langtry explained, "for me to tell how my gowns will look when I am on the stage."

It was continually reiterated in the Press that Mrs. Langtry wore no make-up, but that, Cassandra saw, was untrue.

She deliberately contrived a very pale appearance by using only the faintest touch of rouge on her cheeks, and a powder which was sold in the shops with her name on it.

She out-lined her eyes, darkened her eye-lashes and eye-brows, and finally used a lip-salve sparingly on her mouth.

Cassandra was particularly interested because in the carriage on the way to the theatre, despite Hannah's horrified protests, she had added a touch of colour to her hips and also used powder on her cheeks.

"Whatever are you doing, Miss Cassandra?" Hannah had exclaimed in a tone of horror. "What will people be thinking of you if they see you painted like an actress."

"I am supposed to be an actress," Cassandra had answered.

"And that's nothing to boast about!" Hannah snapped.

"I have an uneasy suspicion that your sentiments are echoed by the majority of the public," Cassandra answered.

Then she closed her ears to the long impassioned recitation of Hannah's disapproval.

Now she noted how skilfully Mrs. Langtry enhanced her appearance while remaining both ladylike and overwhelmingly beautiful.

Finally, a quarter of an hour before the curtain was due to rise, Mr. Frederick Gebhard arrived.

Cassandra remembered reading that this young American had returned with Mrs. Langtry from New York.

Some of her father's more disreputable papers, which she was not supposed to read, such as "*The Sporting Times*" known as "the Pink 'Un", had made some pointed remarks concerning the amount of money the man they called a "Boudoir–Carriage Romeo" had spent on Mrs. Langtry.

Freddy Gebhard who had been bowled over by Lily Langtry's beauty the first night they met, was four years younger than she was.

He was the son of a dry goods businessman, who had left him a yearly income of between eighty and ninety thousand dollars.

Tall, clean shaven and elegant, his Fifth Avenue tailors rated him as New York's "Best Dressed Man", but he bought most of his clothes, which were always dark in colour, in London.

Freddy Gebhard had made the headlines by not only giving Lily Langtry his cheque book, but defending her physically against any admirer who tried to force his acquaintance upon her.

He had knocked out a man who had tried to introduce himself to Lily in St. Louis, and he was lionised by the local bloods during the rest of the week.

He had almost as much Press coverage in the American papers as Lily herself, and by the time Gebhard had gone with her on tour in a private railway-car he had built to her design, he was determined to marry her.

The railway-car advertised his infatuation. It was seventy feet long, painted blue, emblazoned with wreathes of golden lilies, encircling the name 'Lalee'. Brass lilies decorated the roof.

The bath and bathroom fittings were in solid silver.

Lily had returned to England three years earlier in 1883 to try to persuade Mr. Langtry into giving her a divorce but her husband had categorically refused.

She had re-crossed the Atlantic to discover Freddy Gebhard still adored her. He installed her in a luxurious house in West 23rd Street, where they threw riotous parties which were headlined in all the newspapers.

Cassandra thought Freddy Gebhard had a rather weak face. At the same time he was undoubtedly good looking.

He shook her hand politely when they were introduced, but it was obvious that he had eyes only for Mrs. Langtry and was in fact wildly and overwhelmingly in love.

"Lily, my darling, you look more wonderful than I can tell you," he said softly and bent his head to kiss her hand.

'How sad they cannot be married,' was Cassandra's first thought.

Then she thought it strange that a married woman, even if she was an actress, could be on such intimate terms with another man.

Mrs. Langtry appeared, however, to be concerned only with her own appearance and her audience which awaited her in the theatre.

"Every seat is sold out!" Freddy announced.

"But of course!" Lily replied. "They told me when I arrived that people have been queuing since twelve o'clock this morning."

She was already wearing the dress in which she was to appear in the first act.

Cassandra noticed how tightly it was molded over her bosom and how the bustle at the back accentuated her tiny waist.

"You are so lovely," she said impulsively. "It is not surprising everyone wants to see you."

Mrs. Langtry smiled.

"Thank you," she said with the ease of a woman who takes her compliments for granted.

Then turning to Freddy she said:

"Take Miss Standish to the Box, Freddy. She will sit with you during the performance, and then I have promised her we will take her with us to Lord Carwen's party."

"Yes, of course — delighted!" Freddy agreed.

Cassandra felt that he was disappointed that he would not be alone with his adored Lily, and resented the fact that she would accompany them even the short distance from the theatre to where the party was to take place.

"I hope I am not being a nuisance," she said humbly.

She knew even as she spoke that she did not care if she was, for she had every intention of going to the party where there was a chance she would be introduced to the Duke.

"No, of course not," Freddy said politely but with an obvious insincerity.

He kissed both Lily's hands and whispered something in her ear, before he escorted Cassandra down the long draughty passages and through the pass-door, which lay behind the stage, at the side of the auditorium.

An attendant ushered them into the stage-box.

For the first time Cassandra wondered apprehensively if there was anyone in the audience who might recognise her.

It was unlikely. Nevertheless, if any of her friends had come to London from Yorkshire, they would undoubtedly wish to see Mrs. Langtry's play.

Cassandra was well aware of the scandal it would arouse if she were seen alone with a man in the stage-box of a theatre — most of all if she was accompanied by someone as notorious as Freddy Gebhard.

She solved the problem by moving to a seat against the partition so that, while she had the best view of the stage she was almost invisible to the audience.

If Freddy Gebhard thought it strange that she did not wish to make herself conspicuous, he did not say so.

He was only too pleased to take the centre of the Box.

He stood in the front of it looking at the audience, waving to a friend or two in the Stalls, looking up at the Gallery, until finally the people in the cheap seats realised who he was and started to clap.

This was obviously what he was waiting for; for he bowed, waved his hand and was almost childishly elated with his reception.

He sat down and said to Cassandra:

"They are beginning to know me as well over here as they do in New York. I have often said to Lily — we make a splendid pair!"

Cassandra smiled at him.

There was no need for her to say much. He was clearly content with his own appreciation of himself, and once again he bent forward so that the audience could have a good look at him.

Cassandra was glad when the curtain rose.

The play was well-written, thoroughly dramatic and depicted a feud between two older members of a respected aristocratic family and a reconciliation brought about by the love of two younger ones.

In the fourth act Mrs. Langtry had to go on her knees and plead with her father to abandon his foolish schemes and save the old house.

Here, almost to Cassandra's surprise, Lily Langtry proved herself a quite moving actress and she certainly carried the sympathy of the audience with her.

She was very touching when she cried:

"Help us! help us! You are our last and only hope. We give up everything — but save, oh save my brother Percy!"

The applause rang out, the women in the audience wiped their eyes and there was curtain call after curtain call.

A great number of bouquets were carried onto the stage. Lily held in her arms one of the yellow roses which Cassandra guessed had been given her by Freddy.

After "God Save the Queen" Freddy hurried Cassandra back through the stage-door and they waited in the dressing-room, while Mrs. Langtry changed.

She came from behind the curtains wearing a grey satin evening-gown.

There was a necklace of enormous diamonds around her neck and diamonds glittered in her ears and around her wrists.

"Do I look all right?" she asked Freddy.

Cassandra saw him draw in his breath before he answered:

"You are more beautiful every time I look at you!"

"Then let us go to the party," Mrs. Langtry exclaimed, gaily. "Everyone who matters in the theatre world will be there and I have no wish for any of them to eclipse me!"

"No-one could do that!" Freddy said.

He kissed her shoulder passionately as if they were alone and Cassandra was not watching and feeling somewhat embarrassed.

She had sent her own carriage with Hannah to the flat she had rented in Bury Street.

"I'm not going to that place," Hannah said angrily.

"Yes, you are!" Cassandra replied, "unless you wish me to come home alone in a hired cab, and goodness knows then what might happen to me!"

There was nothing Hannah could do after that but agree.

"Send the carriage away," Cassandra told her. "We shall have to find a cab, but doubtless there is a night-porter who will get one for us."

She had also told Hannah to wait for half an hour after she had gone into the theatre before driving away.

There had always been the chance that Mrs. Langtry would accept the present and make arrangements for her to meet the Duke some other night.

Cassandra could only hope the meeting would not be too long delayed, but it seemed, she thought excitedly, as if everything was falling into place.

It was just luck there was a theatrical party that evening and that Mrs. Langtry had been pleased with the present which she thought had been sent to her by Sir James.

In Freddy Gebhard's comfortable carriage, as they moved down the Strand, Cassandra said to herself:

'This is where my play begins! The curtain is rising and I can only pray that I shall give a convincing performance.'

Chapter Four

Lord Carwen's house was in Arlington Street and overlooked Green Park.

It was extremely impressive with a porticoed front-door and iron railings dividing the short drive-in from the pavement.

Cassandra entered behind Mrs. Langtry, and as she saw the brilliantly-lit chandeliers and the luxurious furniture which decorated the hall, she wondered a little apprehensively if there would be anyone at the party who would recognise her.

As she followed in the wake of Lily Langtry, she could see them both reflected in huge, gilt-framed mirrors, and she thought it would be difficult for them to remain unnoticed however large or important the party might be.

Mrs. Langtry's grey gown from the front made her look like a Greek goddess and at the back she had a huge bustle supported by a satin bow which formed the small train.

Despite the wealth of diamonds around her neck and glittering in her hair and on her bodice, she looked both dignified and a lady.

Cassandra could not think the same about herself.

Her dress from Chasemore was lovely in its own way, but she knew she would never have dared to wear it as Cassandra Sherburn.

Of vivid green, almost as deep as an emerald, it was fashioned of tulle, ruched round the extremely low neck and over her shoulders.

The colour made her skin look strikingly white, whilst the very tight bodice revealed the curves of her young figure and her very small waist.

Tulle fashioned the enormous bustle even bigger than Mrs. Langtry's — which billowed out behind her, cascading down in frill upon frill to the floor.

But what made the dress different from the type of gown Cassandra would have worn as herself was the fact that the tulle was strewn with tiny silver and green sequins which glittered and shimmered with every move she made.

It was also caught up at one side with an enormous bunch of artificial water lilies, and these too were speckled with sequins which looked at a distance as if they were dew-drops glistening in the light.

It was a gown that a leading lady could

have worn for her entrance in the first Act, and would undoubtedly have stimulated a round of applause.

Cassandra had with some difficulty persuaded Hannah to arrange her hair in innumerable curls on top of her head, and amongst them she wore three diamond combs.

She also wore diamond ear-rings which she had been left by her Grandmother, but which on a young girl Sir James had thought too sophisticated.

There was the sound of music and then, just before they reached the Reception-room, Cassandra had a last glimpse of herself in the mirror and smiled.

Her red lips certainly contributed to the flamboyance of her appearance. She had applied a little more salve to them in the dressing-room while she was waiting for Mrs. Langtry to change after the performance.

Her eyes did not need any additional artifice since her lashes were naturally so long and dark and, because she was excited at what was happening, her eyes shone even more brightly than the sequins on her dress or the diamonds in her hair.

"Lily! Shall I say how overjoyed I am to see your beautiful face?" a deep voice exclaimed.

A man of about forty, rather large and overpowering, was raising Mrs. Langtry's hand to his lips.

"I have brought a little friend with me," Mrs. Langtry said. "I hope you do not mind?"

Cassandra felt the man's eyes take in every detail of her face and her sensational gown.

"But of course, I am delighted," Lord Carwen said. "Will you introduce me?"

"Miss Sandra Standish," Mrs. Langtry said. "And this, dear, is your very kind and generous host — Lord Carwen!"

Cassandra made a graceful curtsey.

"I hope Your Lordship will forgive me for coming uninvited to your party," she said with a smile.

"I am prepared to forgive you anything, if you will dance with me later," Lord Carwen replied.

He held out his hand to Freddy Gebhard.

"Delighted to see you, Freddy. I hope my party measures up to some of those which I hear you gave in America."

Cassandra did not listen for Mr. Gebhard's reply.

She was staring round the Ball-room, her eyes alight with curiosity.

It was a beautiful room with huge chandeliers and decorated with fabulous pictures and very valuable mirrors.

It was in fact the type of room Cassandra had seen often enough in the homes of her father's friends, but it was the occupants on this occasion who were unusual.

The men were all gentlemen, the majority of them of Lord Carwen's age.

Many of them were obviously distinguished and they had an elegance which could be achieved only by an Englishman in evening-dress.

But the women were to Cassandra's eyes quite fantastic!

'It is extraordinary,' she thought, 'to see so many pretty women all together!'

Then she realised it was because, using cosmetics, they looked far prettier and far more attractive than their contemporaries in the social world who dared not employ such means to beautify themselves.

Eyes enlarged with mascara and eye-shadow, very pink and white skins, and laughing red lips made a picture which Cassandra could understand most men would find alluring and desirable.

Their gowns too were fashioned to attract attention.

Never had she seen so much naked flesh, such yards of tulle, so many sequins, or such a profusion of artificial flowers.

The majority of the women wore jewellery which Cassandra could tell at a glance was not real.

Nevertheless, it added to the glamour of their appearance.

She was so amused and interested in everything she saw that she gave a start when she heard Mrs. Langtry say beside her:

"As I expected, I see the Duke of Alchester over there. Let me introduce him, otherwise we may become separated in the crowd and then I should not have been able to keep my promise to you."

Cassandra drew in her breath.

Mrs. Langtry swept ahead of her, and once again she followed in the wake of the grey bustle, moving through the throng of guests who seemed to be talking animatedly at the top of their voices, or laughing with a kind of wild gaiety which almost shook the chandeliers.

For a moment Cassandra felt that she could not look at the Duke.

She felt a sudden shyness creep over her. She wanted to run away. Then she told herself she was being ridiculous.

This was what she had planned — this was what she had schemed and dreamed about. Now it was up to her!

It was certainly not a moment for shyness or embarrassment. She had to convince the Duke that she was a gay, rather pushing young actress.

She had to amuse him . . . to make him notice her!

Mrs. Langtry had stopped, and now Cassandra saw him, the man who had been in her thoughts ever since she was twelve.

He was far better-looking than his pictures suggested. He was no longer the thin, rather cadaverous boy she remembered in his white flannels and Eton-blue cap at Lords.

He was tall, broad-shouldered, and had an almost commanding presence which she had not expected.

She had somehow not imagined that he would have such natural dignity or would have a pride in his bearing which she sensed immediately.

It was obvious even in the grace with which he rose from the chair on which he was sitting to greet Mrs. Langtry.

"I expected to find you here, Varro," Mrs. Langtry said.

"I am honoured that you should think of me," the Duke answered.

As he spoke, Cassandra knew that she remembered his voice. There was some quality in it which she had never heard from anyone else — something she, in particular, found strangely moving.

"You have not been to see me in my new Play," Mrs. Langtry said accusingly.

"I assure you that it is only because I have found it impossible to obtain a seat," the Duke replied.

Cassandra watching him realised that his eyes twinkled as he spoke and when he smiled there was a dimple on the left side of his mouth.

'He is wildly, overwhelmingly attractive,' she told herself, 'much more so than I had imagined! There cannot be a woman in the whole of London who would not try to marry him if he so much as looked in her direction!'

"You should not be so popular!" the Duke was saying to Mrs. Langtry. "They tell me there have never been such long queues as I see outside the Prince's day after day."

"You should have seen them in America," Freddy Gebhard interposed, who had followed Mrs. Langtry and Cassandra across the room.

"Hello, Freddy!" the Duke exclaimed. "When are you going to find time to come and have a drink with me at White's?"

"The next time that Lily doesn't want

me," Freddy Gebhard replied.

"But I always want you," Lily Langtry said softly.

"Then I withdraw my invitation," the Duke said. "Who am I to interfere between two people who obviously enjoy each other's company?"

He spoke quite seriously, but Cassandra could see that his eyes were laughing.

"And now, Varro," Mrs. Langtry said, "I have someone with me who is very anxious to meet you. She has something to tell you which I expect you will find interesting."

She turned towards Cassandra.

"Miss Standish, may I present the Duke of Alchester? Varro — this is Miss Sandra Standish, who I understand is an extremely talented young woman."

Cassandra put out her hand and, as the Duke took it, she had the strangest feeling that all this had happened before.

She could not explain it to herself. It was as if they were enacting an episode which had taken place, not once, but a dozen times, all down the ages.

"You have something to tell me?" the Duke said raising his eye-brows.

"Yes," Cassandra answered and she was relieved to hear that her voice did not quiver. "But at the moment it would be impossible to make myself heard."

Even as she spoke, the Band which had been playing when they first arrived in the hall, started up again.

It was a waltz and Freddy Gebhard said to Mrs. Langtry:

"This is one of our tunes."

He did not wait for a reply, but put his arm round her and led her on to the centre of the room.

The Duke and Cassandra stood alone, facing each other.

"Will you dance with me first?" he asked.

"I would like that."

She felt herself quiver as he put an arm round her and hoped he would not notice.

Then he was swinging her round the floor and she found he was easy to dance with and they seemed to be perfectly matched.

If she had wanted to talk to him, it would have been impossible.

The noise and laughter from the other guests was quite deafening, and the Band played louder than was usual at other parties which Cassandra had attended.

The dance was by no means decorous even for a waltz. It was in fact quite riotous and as it ended Cassandra moved from the floor to the other end of the room which seemed a little less crowded.

"Let us find somewhere where we can sit down," the Duke suggested.

He put his hand under her arm with a lack of formality in which she knew he would not have indulged at a more formal Ball.

He led her out through a door, and she saw there were various Drawing-rooms and Ante-rooms leading off the room in which they had been dancing.

There was one which she guessed was a Writing-room, beautifully decorated in soft colours with French furniture which must have been worth a fortune.

There was a sofa in front of the curtained window, the lights were discreetly low and there was the fragrance of hot-house flowers to scent the atmosphere.

The Duke led Cassandra to the sofa, and when she had seated herself he sat beside her, turning a little sideways so that he would look into her face.

"Who are you?" he asked, "and why have we never met before?"

"Surely that is a very conventional remark for someone like you?" Cassandra replied.

"Why for me in particular?"

"Because you have the reputation of being original, dashing and very intelligent."

128

"Good Heavens!" The Duke held up his hands in pretended horror. "Who has been telling you such a lot of lies about me?"

"In my profession," Cassandra replied, "they chatter about you almost as much as they do about the productions in which they hope to appear."

"I think you are being rather unkind to me," the Duke said accusingly, but his eyes were twinkling. "Have I done anything to offend you?"

"On the contrary," Cassandra said. "As Mrs. Langtry told you, I was very anxious to meet you."

"Why?"

Cassandra hesitated a moment and then she said:

"For one frivolous reason and one serious one. Which will you have first?"

"The frivolous one!" the Duke replied. "At this sort of party one never wants to be serious."

"Well . . . the frivolous reason is that I have often wondered why someone as gifted as you are should find the theatre more amusing than anything else."

She realised as she spoke she was being deliberately provocative.

Yet she knew she had to hold his attention, to make him curious about her, or else she might lose him as quickly as she had found him.

"How do you know that?" he asked.

Cassandra laughed.

"Are you really surprised that I can read?"

"You mean the newspapers! You should never believe all you read in those scurrilous rags."

"Nevertheless, they cannot invent all the things they say about you," Cassandra said. "I read for instance that you attained a First Class Degree at Oxford and that at one time you considered a career in the Diplomatic Service. That must mean that you are able to speak several languages."

"That was a long time ago," the Duke answered. "I suppose I was ambitious once, but then I decided it was all too much trouble."

"I think people are happier when they are working at something which interests them."

"Is that what you found?"

"I am always interested in what I am doing," Cassandra answered truthfully.

"Tell me about yourself."

"What do you want to know?"

"Are you acting at the moment?"

"No, I have come South to London for singing lessons. There is a chance of my getting a good part in a Musical Comedy, but

130

my voice is not yet strong enough and I have to work hard at it for at least a month."

"Who has arranged all this for you?"

It was a question Cassandra had not expected and she had to think for a moment before she replied:

"A . . . friend has given me an introduction to a good teacher."

As soon as she spoke she saw the Duke's eyes glance at the diamonds in her ears and in her hair and she wondered if he thought a man had paid for them.

She felt the blood rising in her cheeks and a little ripple of fear run through her in case the Duke should be shocked.

Then she told herself not to worry: it was what he would expect from anyone in the theatre-world.

Had her father not said that men liked giving presents to actresses they took out to supper?

"So you are spending a month in London," the Duke said reflectively. "Will you be very busy all of the time?"

She smiled at him.

"I am always ready to be . . . tempted into playing truant."

"They tell me that is a part I play extremely well," the Duke said. "Will you come to the theatre with me one night?"

"I would enjoy that," Cassandra said simply. "I had not been to a theatre in London for a very long time until tonight when I saw 'Enemies'."

"What did you think of it?"

"I think Mrs. Langtry was magnificent in the part."

"She is extremely adaptable," the Duke said.

Then, as if Mrs. Langtry did not particularly interest him, he went on:

"Now will you tell me the serious reason why you wanted to meet me?"

Cassandra had her story ready. She had thought it all out coming down to London in the train.

"Do you remember a groom your father once had with the name of 'Abbey'?"

There was a little frown of concentration between the Duke's eyes.

"Do you mean a man who was at Alchester many years ago when I was a child?"

"That would be Abbey," Cassandra replied. "I knew him when he was very old. I used to visit him in the cottage to which he retired."

"Of course, I remember old Abbey!" the Duke exclaimed. "Even when I was a child his face was like a withered walnut. He must have been a hundred when you knew him."

"He was eighty-seven before he died," Cassandra said. "He asked me just before his last illness to tell you, if we ever met, that he still had the horseshoe that you gave him."

"Good Heavens!" the Duke exclaimed. "I remember the incident well! Abbey was an inveterate gambler. He never had a penny to his name and he was always full of stories of how his horse had been 'pipped at the post'."

"Yes, I heard them too," Cassandra said with a little smile.

"One day when he was taking me out riding," the Duke went on, "we stopped for a rest and I was running around, as small boys do, and found a discarded horseshoe.

" 'Look Abbey,' I cried, 'I have found a horseshoe.'

" 'So you have, Master Varro,' he replied. 'It'll bring you luck.'

"I remember debating with myself for a moment, because I wanted to take the horseshoe back home to show my father, but then I said:

" 'I think you need luck more than I do, Abbey,' and I gave it to him."

"That is exactly the same story that he told me," Cassandra said with a little cry of delight. "The horseshoe stood on his mantelpiece right up to the day of his death. It was in the place of honour and I think it did bring him luck."

"I have not thought of Abbey for years," the Duke said. "I have an idea he went to work for a racehorse owner called Sir James Sherburn. Is that right?"

"He may have," Cassandra said lightly. "When I knew him he was far too old to work. He talked of nothing but horses."

"And what could be a better subject?" the Duke enquired. "Except of course, beautiful women!"

There was no disguising the expression in his eyes.

"I believe you are an acknowledged judge of both," Cassandra answered.

"Again you flatter me," the Duke answered. "Shall I tell you I cannot resist a fine horse or a lovely woman, and you are very lovely, Miss Standish!"

Cassandra could not prevent the blush rising in her cheeks, and for a moment her eye-lashes flickered shyly. Then she forced herself to say:

"Your Grace is obviously also an expert flatterer."

"You say that with a cynical note in your voice which I do not like!" he said accusingly. "How can I convince you that I am

134

sincere? Surely in the North, or wherever you come from, there must be men who have eyes in their heads and are not completely blind?"

"They can see with their eyes," Cassandra answered, "but perhaps they are not quite so glib with their tongues as you gentlemen in the South!"

The Duke threw back his head and laughed.

"You have an answer to everything. Come, let us go and dance and I hope that as you are a stranger to London you do not know many other men here tonight."

"As a matter of fact, I am throwing myself on your mercy," Cassandra answered, "as I do not wish to keep bothering Mrs. Langtry for introductions."

"There is no need for that," the Duke said firmly. "I will look after you, and that is something at which I can assure you, without boasting, I am very proficient!"

The dance-floor was even more crowded than when they had left it, but the Duke skilfully steered them round the room and Cassandra wondered how she had ever enjoyed dancing in the past.

It was something quite different to be held in the Duke's arms; to feel her hand in his and know the tulle trimming her *décolletage* brushed against the satin facing of his evening-coat.

"You dance divinely!" he said. "Do you dance on the stage?"

"I am a better . . . actress," Cassandra replied.

The party was getting even noisier than it had been in the earlier part of the evening, and now as the dance came to an end the Band started up the loud gay music which heralded the 'Can-Can'.

"We will watch this," the Duke said. "It is always amusing."

Cassandra had read in her father's sporting papers of how the Can-Can had startled London some years before.

Brought from Paris by a *troupe* consisting of two men and a girl, who were brothers and sister, they appeared at The Oxford Music Hall, and packed the place night after night.

The Can-Can was considered the very height of impropriety and even "*The Sporting Times*" had some very scathing things to say about it.

Cassandra did not read this paper bought by her father, because she was not interested in the 'seamy' side of London, nor in the broad jokes which she did not understand.

She read it because, so often, the Duke, as the Marquis of Charlbury was mentioned in it.

Every few months or so "*The Sporting Times*" gave a list of what they called "The Young Bloods About Town".

It also referred to the "Mashers" who haunted the stage-door of the Gaiety and were to be found at "the promenades" of all the Music Halls.

Cassandra added cuttings which mentioned the Marquis to her Album, but when she was searching for his name it was impossible not to be interested in the theatre gossip with which she realised he was so closely connected.

The Can-Can was later to lose the Alhambra its licence because of the slim legs and high kicks of a young lady called "Wiry Sal".

Cassandra had often wondered exactly what it was like and now she was to find out!

Quite a number of Lord Carwen's female guests considered they were proficient at the dance which had been denounced even in Paris because it revealed what women wore under their skirts — and what they did not wear!

It was obvious that the ladies of Lord Carwen's party wore extremely frilly and lacy underclothes.

Amid the roars of applause from the Gentlemen guests present, they kicked their legs and went on kicking them round and round the room.

Cheeks became flushed, hair became loosened, but the high kicks went on with more and more frothy underclothes being revealed until, despite every resolution, Cassandra found herself really shocked.

The Duke was looking amused, but he was not cheering and shouting like the other men, who endeavored to incite the girls to kick their legs even higher and be even more daring than they were already.

She felt she could not go on looking at members of her own sex making such disgusting exhibitions of themselves. She felt as if she too was degraded because she was a woman.

"It is very . . . hot," she murmured and turned away from the dance floor towards a window.

The Duke followed her.

Cassandra stood looking out into the darkness of the Park. She could just see the branches of the trees silhouetted against the sky.

"You have never seen the Can-Can before?" the Duke asked.

"No."

"You are surprised? It is not what you expected?"

"No."

"I have the feeling you are shocked," he said, his eyes on Cassandra's averted face.

"It . . . seems somewhat . . . abandoned," she faltered.

"I understand. I do not expect that such extravagances have yet reached the North."

"No."

Behind them the dancers had collapsed into chairs around the ballroom and even onto the floor itself, panting and exhausted. Now the Band changed from the exuberant music to a soft, dreamy waltz.

Cassandra looked at the Duke expecting him to invite her once again onto the floor, when a voice beside her said:

"You promised me a dance, pretty lady!"

She glanced up and saw Lord Carwen standing beside them.

"I hope Varro has been entertaining you," Lord Carwen said, "while I was regretfully too busy to do so."

"He has been very kind," Cassandra murmured.

"And now I must see if I can equal or even excel his kindness," Lord Carwen said.

He drew Cassandra into his arms and they began to dance.

She realised that he was holding her too closely and too tightly. When she tried to move a little further away from him, he merely laughed down at her.

"You are very lovely, Sandra."

She felt herself stiffen at his familiar use of her Christian name, then told herself it was out of character.

"You have a lovely house, My Lord."

"I'm not interested in my house, but in the loveliest person in it," he replied. "Lily Langtry tells me you have just come to London. You must allow me to show you some of the amusements."

"Thank you," Cassandra answered, "but I am afraid I shall be very busy with my singing lessons."

Lord Carwen laughed.

"It does not matter whether you sing or not," he said. "You only have to look as you look now and you will fill the theatre for a thousand nights!"

He paused and added:

"That is, if the theatre is really important to you. I can think of more interesting things to do."

"And what could they be?" Cassandra asked without really considering what his answer was likely to be.

"That is something I can explain to you in

great detail," Lord Carwen said tightening his arm around her waist.

As he did so Cassandra realised that she disliked him.

It was not only because he was treating her in a familiar manner — that was her own fault, she had invited it upon herself.

But there was something unpleasant about him as a man, and she was a good judge of people.

Even as a child she had seldom been wrong in judging the character or the characteristics of the people who came to The Towers and Sir James had encouraged this perceptiveness.

"How did that man strike you?" he would ask when someone had come to luncheon or for dinner. "What did you think of that fellow?"

Sometimes Cassandra would say:

"He is all right. Rather stupid, I thought."

But occasionally she said:

"Have nothing to do with him, Papa. I am sure he is crooked! There is something about him I mistrust."

Over the years Sir James found she was invariably right.

Once he came to her to say:

"You remember that man you warned me against, who came here about six months ago? His name was Bull."

"Yes, I remember," Cassandra answered. "There was something about him I mistrusted."

"He has just received a sentence of eight years at the Old Bailey for fraud."

Cassandra knew that she was not wrong now. There was something about Lord Carwen which made her involuntarily wince away from him.

"Will you dine with me tomorrow night?" he asked. "I want to talk to you."

There was something in his tone which told her that conversation was not his main objective.

"Thank you but I have an engagement." He smiled.

"Are you playing hard-to-get, little Sandra? I assure you I am very persistent, and I know we are going to see a great deal of each other."

"Do you give many parties like this?" she asked in an effort to try and change the conversation.

"I will give any sort of party you wish me to give," Lord Carwen replied. "Ask Varro. He will tell you I am a very agreeable Host, and very generous to those I — like."

The Band stopped playing.

"Thank-you for our dance," Cassandra said.

She would have been unable to move away from him because Lord Carwen still kept his arm around her waist, if at that moment some new arrivals had not diverted His Lordship's attention.

Quickly Cassandra hurried away.

She was relieved to find that the Duke had not taken another partner but was standing alone, leaning against a pillar at the far end of the room.

She almost ran towards him.

As if he knew instinctively that she had not enjoyed her dance he said:

"Shall we go and find the supper-room? Or better still, shall we slip away and I will give you supper somewhere else?"

Cassandra's eyes looked up into his.

"Could we do that?"

"Why not?" he answered. "Come with me. I know another way of reaching the Hall so that we need not embarrass our Host by bidding him good-bye."

Like two conspirators they slipped out of the Ballroom and the Duke led Cassandra through several Reception rooms back to the Hall where guests were still arriving.

"You are not leaving, Varro?" a pretty woman cried putting out her hand towards the Duke.

"I am afraid so."

"How disappointing!"

Two red lips pouted very invitingly.

"I will doubtless be seeing you in the next day or two."

"Come to my dressing-room in the interval and have a drink."

"I will," the Duke promised.

Cassandra stood on one side feeling for the moment forgotten.

Yet she could understand why the Duke found this gay, informal life he had chosen amusing.

So much more so than the type of entertainment to which he received an embossed invitation card and where he must make desultory and stilted conversation.

Also being a Duke, he would always have to escort an old Dowager into supper because she would be of higher social importance than the pretty young girls he would have preferred.

'Of course he finds this more fun,' Cassandra told herself.

She felt despairingly that nothing she could say or do would ever make him think differently.

"Do you mind if we take a hansom? I have only one coachman in London, and he is getting old, so I send him home at about 12 o'clock."

"I would love to go in a hansom," Cassandra answered.

She was well aware it was considered very fast to travel in what Disraeli had called "London's Gondolas".

Her father had once taken her for a drive in one when she was only fifteen, but no young man of her acquaintance would have dared to suggest such a thing.

As the Cabman closed the glass front over them, there was something very intimate in being so close to each other in a tiny, isolated world of their own.

The Duke reached out and took Cassandra's hand.

"I am so glad that you agreed to come away with me," he said. "I want to talk to you! I want to listen to you teasing me with that provocative note in your voice which tells me that you are not quite as impressed with me as you ought to be!"

Cassandra felt herself quiver. The touch of his hand sent little shivers down her spine.

She was thrilling to the warmth of his fingers; to the knowledge that their shoulders were in contact and their faces were very near to each other's.

"You are lovely! Ridiculously and absurdly lovely!" the Duke said and she thought that his tone was sincere. "How could you possibly have blue eyes with that strange, half-red half-gold hair?"

"There must be Irish blood in me somewhere!"

Cassandra felt as if it was difficult to speak. Her throat was contracting so strange little feelings were rippling through her. She could not help wondering if the Duke felt the same.

"Your eye-lashes. Do you darken them?"

Cassandra shook her head.

"They are natural."

"If you are lying to me, I shall wash them and see."

"You can do that. They are what the Irish call 'Blue eyes put in with dirty fingers', and I promise you they will resist rain and tempest. Water is completely ineffective."

"I would still like to try," he said softly.

By the lights shining into the hansom as they passed through Trafalgar Square she could see the look in his eyes.

They had that curious, searching expression that she remembered so well.

"There are so many things I want to ask you and so much I want to hear, and I am delighted beyond words that you did not wish to stay at that noisy party."

As he spoke, he drew her kid glove very

gently from her right hand. Cassandra did not speak because she did not know what to say.

The Duke turned her hand over, as if to look at the palm.

"Such a small and very pretty hand," he said.

As he spoke he pressed his lips on her palm.

Cassandra told herself she ought to stop him; she ought to protest that he must not do such a thing to her! But her voice dried in her throat.

It was a wonder such as she had never known to feel the warm persistence of his mouth and to know deliriously and incredibly her dreams had come true.

Then she remembered it was all play-acting. She was acting and so was he!

This was amusement — this was fun! This was just the bubbles one found in a glass of champagne!

Nothing real, nothing serious, nothing permanent about it, and to forget the truth for one moment would be disastrous.

The Duke released her hand.

"Here we are!" he said. "I thought you would like to go to Romano's."

They seemed to have reached the Strand very quickly.

Cassandra was well aware of how famous

Romano's Restaurant was; she had heard it spoken of so often, but she had never expected it to be as gay as it was.

The oblong room with its dark-red draped curtains and plush sofas was filled with men and women eating supper after the theatres were closed.

Cassandra guessed that many of them were Gaiety Girls, simply because they seemed more attractive, more alluring and far better dressed than the other women.

Nearly every one of them wore flowers in her hair, their *décolletage* was extremely low, their waists so tiny it seemed as if a man's two hands could easily meet round them.

They all appeared to have perfect complexions; they all appeared to be laughing until the whole Restaurant was filled with their gaiety.

Romano himself, a dark, suave little man, greeted the Duke with respectful delight and led them to a sofa underneath the balcony.

As she walked towards it, Cassandra realised that at least three-quarters of the women in the Restaurant knew the Duke and waved and smiled at him whenever they could catch his eye.

There appeared to be flowers everywhere, and she was to learn later that the Gaiety

Girls had special tables kept for them which their admirers decked with flowers. Some sat under a veritable canopy of blooms.

Some had bells of blossoms with their names emblazoned on them suspended over their heads.

It was quite unlike any Restaurant that Cassandra could have imagined, and once again she could understand why the Duke found it amusing.

The sofa on which they sat close together was very comfortable.

The waiter brought them a hand-written menu and the wine-waiter hovered behind him.

"What would you like to eat?" the Duke asked.

"Very little," Cassandra answered. "I am not hungry, but please order for me."

The Duke gave the order and then chose from the wine list a bottle of champagne.

It seemed that the champagne was almost compulsory in Romano's, for huge silver wine-coolers stood beside every table.

Before the night was out, Cassandra saw what she had often read about but hardly believed: champagne being drunk from the white satin slipper of a beautiful young woman whose table was festooned with the most expensive orchids in the room.

Her admirer poured champagne into her shoe and stood up to toast her. The other men in the party raised their glasses.

"Who is that?" Cassandra asked.

The Duke looked at her in surprise.

"Do you really not know?"

"I have no idea."

"That is Connie Gilchrist. You must have heard of her."

"Yes of course I have," Cassandra replied. "I recognise her now from the portrait sketches of her in the illustrated papers, but she is far prettier in real life."

"She is very attractive," the Duke answered, "as half the men in London will tell you."

"Are you in love with her?" Cassandra enquired.

As she spoke she was astonished at her own daring, and yet she felt that in some way she had to arrest his attention by keeping him amused, if only by her boldness.

"No!" he answered.

"Then with whom are you in love?" Cassandra enquired. "Or is that an impertinent question?"

He looked at her, his eyes twinkling.

"You are very direct. You have asked me a lot of intimate questions, and yet you have not answered one of mine. I think it is my turn."

"Very well," Cassandra answered, "what do you want to know?"

"The thing is," the Duke said in rather a strange tone, "I want to know so much that I cannot put into words. I have a feeling there is a great deal behind everything you say. Behind everything we have talked about this evening there is something I do not understand."

Cassandra did not answer and he said:

"I am not explaining myself well, and yet I have the feeling you know what I mean."

"I think you are curious," she said. "When you look at people, you have a curious look in your eyes."

"How do you know that?" he asked sharply. "People have said something of that sort to me before, but we have only just met."

"Yes . . . I know," Cassandra answered.

"I know what you are thinking," he said unexpectedly, "and I believe you feel the same way I do, that we are not strangers to each other."

"Why should we feel like that?" Cassandra answered, without attempting to deny his assertion.

"I do not know," he replied, "but it is something I am determined to find out."

Chapter Five

Cassandra and the Duke sat talking and time seemed to speed by so quickly that it was with genuine surprise she found it was after two o'clock in the morning.

She had never before had a meal alone with a man except her father.

She realised now how much more interesting and indeed entrancing it was to talk intimately with the Duke, to feel the stimulus of his mind and above all, to know that their eyes were saying so much more than their lips actually spoke.

There was no mistaking the admiration in the Duke's expression.

There was something very personal in their conversation, something which made even the most banal subjects somehow seem special to them both.

They talked of horses and the Duke said:

"You sound as if you have ridden quite a lot."

"I have," Cassandra answered.

She saw a question in his eyes and added:

"Perhaps it is easier when one is living in the North than it would be in the South."

"Maybe it is less expensive," the Duke

conceded. "At the same time I am sure wherever you are there will always be men who will wish you to ride their horses."

Cassandra knew he was thinking that an actress would not be able either to afford horses or to have much time for hunting! So she excused herself by saying:

"My father keeps horses."

"Your father lives in the North?"

"Yes."

"I would like to see you on a horse," the Duke said.

Then with a different note in his voice he said:

"Will you come with me to Tattersall's tomorrow?"

"To the Sale-rooms?"

He nodded.

"Tomorrow is Friday," Cassandra said. "I thought as the sales are on Monday, one could only inspect the horses on Sunday."

"That is true for the general public," the Duke answered, "but my horses are arriving at Knightsbridge Green tomorrow morning from my stables in Newmarket and from Alchester Park."

"You are selling them?" Cassandra exclaimed.

"I am selling the last twenty of my father's stud."

She heard the pain in his voice and said impulsively:

"But you must not do that! Your father's horses are famous."

"I have to sell."

"But why?"

There was a twisted smile on his lips as the Duke replied:

"Is not the reason obvious? Why does one have to sell anything that one treasures except for money?"

Cassandra was silent. She could not understand what was happening.

If the Duke thought he was going to marry the rich Miss Sherburn, why should he dispose of his precious horses? She knew from the expression on his face that they meant as much to him as they had to his father.

The Alchester Stud was famous, and the late Duke in the last years of his life had won a great number of races.

He had also been a notable Patron of the Turf, a member of the Jockey Club, and was so popular that whenever he appeared on a race-course he was cheered by the crowds.

It seemed incredible to Cassandra that the new Duke should dispose of the Stud that had taken his father a life-time to build up and on which he had expended not only money but loving care.

She was finding it difficult not to ask the questions that were trembling on her lips when the Duke went on:

"I would like you to see my horses. It will be the last time that I shall look at them, except perhaps when they are racing under someone else's colours. I could not bear to attend the sale on Monday."

"I can understand that," Cassandra said. "But surely if you need money so badly, there is something else you can sell?"

"Do you suppose I have not thought of that?" he asked almost sharply. "No, there is nothing."

It seemed to Cassandra as he spoke that he withdrew from her, so that for the first time that evening they were no longer close and friendly, but strangers.

Then the party which included Connie Gilchrist rose to leave the Restaurant.

The women's voices were so loud and shrill as they said good-night to each other that it was impossible to go on talking until they had moved down the Restaurant towards the door.

Connie Gilchrist however turned back and walked towards the Duke.

He rose to his feet as she approached.

"How are you, Varro?" she asked. "I've not seen you this last week."

"I have been out of London as it happens," the Duke replied. "I only returned this evening — too late to come to the Theatre."

"We all wondered what had happened to you," Connie Gilchrist said.

She was blond, very pink and white and attractive, Cassandra thought, but her voice was not as pretty as her face. There was something slightly harsh about it, and just a touch of commonness in the way she pronounced some of her words.

"I'll see you tomorrow evening, I hope," Connie said. "Good-night, Varro."

"Good-night, Connie," he replied.

She hurried after her friends, an exaggerated bustle of pink satin rustling behind her.

The Duke re-seated himself beside Cassandra.

"I did not introduce you," he said. "Did you wish to meet her?"

"I am quite content to admire her from afar," Cassandra answered.

"She is a great draw," the Duke said. "I will take you to the Gaiety one evening; it will amuse you."

"Thank you," Cassandra replied.

The Duke signaled to the wine-waiter who filled up their glasses.

Cassandra began to think that she ought

to suggest leaving, and yet she could not bear the evening to come to an end.

Perhaps tomorrow the Duke would regret the various invitations he had given her. Perhaps he would not find her so interesting or so attractive as he had appeared to do earlier in the evening.

Since they had talked of his horses it seemed as if his mood had changed.

'I must try to think of a way to amuse him,' Cassandra told herself.

Then as she was frantically searching for a new subject, the Duke said:

"What do you think about when you are acting?"

Cassandra considered for a moment.

"When I am playing a part," she answered, "I am trying to think of the effect it will have on the people who are listening to me."

This was the truth, she thought. For she had not thought of herself during the evening, but solely of the impression she was making on the Duke.

"That is not the answer most actors and actresses give," the Duke said. "They usually say that they think themselves into the role they have to play so that in fact they become the person they depict."

"I suppose that is how it should be," Cassandra said.

"They are lucky!" the Duke exclaimed. "Actors and actresses can play a rôle, and then discard it. When they leave the stage, they can become themselves. They do not have to go on pretending!"

There was a note in his voice that told Cassandra that he was speaking personally.

"I think what you are trying to say," she said slowly, her eyes on his face, "is that the people who are not on the stage have to go on acting indefinitely."

She smiled and continued:

"Have you forgotten that Shakespeare said — 'All the world's a stage and all the men and women merely players'?"

"That may be true," the Duke said, "but the trouble is the play goes on too long. There is no escape. Only actors and actresses can change their roles and, as I have said, are free to be themselves."

"Do you really think that is so desirable?" Cassandra asked. "I think actors and actresses are mimics and, if they are really professional, they have to subordinate their own personalities to the part they are playing. If not, they become even on the stage, like so many of our famous actors, themselves . . . very thinly disguised."

"What do you mean by that?" the Duke asked.

"If an actor has any personality," Cassandra answered, "he is not Julius Caesar, Bottom, or, if you like, a crossing-Sweeper or a Policeman. Instead, he is Martin Harvey, or Beerbohm Tree in that particular part, and one can never really forget the person beneath the trappings."

She paused and went on:

"Just as when I watched Mrs. Langtry tonight, I was not thinking of the miserable, unhappy woman trying to save her brother, but how skilfully Lily Langtry was pretending to be her."

"I have never thought of it that way," the Duke said slowly.

"Can you not see that a good actress should have as little character or personality of her own as possible?" Cassandra continued. "Then when you watch her in a part you are not distracted by the knowledge that she herself is doing it."

"You are destroying my illusions about the stage," the Duke said accusingly.

"I think that you are envious merely of actors because you are bored with your own part," Cassandra said daringly.

"Who would want to play the Duke?" he asked bitterly.

"A great number of people," Cassandra answered, "and actually it is a hero's rôle.

How much you make yourself a real hero is up to you."

"Do you really believe that?"

"Of course I believe it! If we are assuming as we have been, that we each have in life a special part to play, a Lawyer must be a Lawyer, that is his profession. But whether he is a good or bad one is up to him!"

She went on:

"The same applies to a Salesman or Labourer or a Duke! I think in life we cannot often alter our rôle, but we *can* improve the performance!"

The Duke looked at her for a long moment and then he said:

"You are a very remarkable person, Sandra. You have given me a lot to think about. Something I certainly did not expect to happen this evening!"

"What did you expect?"

The Duke paused for a moment as if he considered his words.

"I expected to be amused, beguiled, captivated. You are, as you are well aware, one of the loveliest people I have ever seen."

"Again you speak as an expert?" Cassandra smiled.

"Of course!" he answered. "But now you have opened new vistas, unlocked doors that I had thought were closely shut. How shall I describe the effect you are having upon me?"

There was an expression in his eyes that made Cassandra feel shy.

She saw that while they had been talking the Restaurant had been emptying and now there were only a few couples like themselves left, and the waiters were yawning.

"I think . . . I should go . . . home," she said.

"I suppose we must," the Duke answered reluctantly.

He asked for the bill.

Cassandra sent for her wrap and they walked towards the entrance. Romano was waiting with a bunch of pink roses in his hand.

"May I ask you to accept these?" he said to Cassandra. "His Grace has brought many beautiful women to my Restaurant, but tonight you have eclipsed them all."

"Thank you," Cassandra said a little shyly.

She took the roses, a doorman called a hackney-carriage and the Duke assisted her into it.

"Tomorrow, if you will dine with me," he said, "I will try to produce a vehicle more worthy of you. I am ashamed that tonight I must treat you in such a shabby fashion."

"It has been a wonderful evening," Cassandra said softly.

The cab smelt of hay, old leather and horse.

But it was close and intimate to be sitting next to the Duke and she knew as he put his arm around her shoulder that he was thinking the same thing.

She felt a thrill run through her! Then as he drew her closer and she realised he was about to kiss her, she turned her head away.

"No!"

"No?" he questioned. "I want to kiss you, Sandra, I want it more than I can possibly tell you."

"We have . . . only just . . . met," Cassandra murmured.

It was difficult to speak sensibly with his arm touching her.

She had a feeling of weakness she had never known before, a weakness combined with a kind of wild excitement which made it hard to think clearly.

"I feel I have known you for a very long time," the Duke said in his deep voice. "I feel too that we were meant to meet. There is something inevitable about it."

Cassandra did not speak and after a moment he said:

"You are so lovely, and so completely and

absolutely different from anyone I have ever met before."

He gave a little laugh.

"You will tell me that it sounds banal, and yet it is true. I cannot explain it in words, but I know that this is different."

"In what . . . way?" Cassandra asked.

"That is something I intend to explain to you, but not tonight."

The Duke's arm tightened.

"You tell me not to kiss you, but I have the feeling, Sandra, that if I insisted you would not resist me."

Cassandra felt a little quiver run through her at his words. He felt it too.

"But because this *is* different," he went on, "because I want you to think of me in a very special way, I will not kiss you until you allow me to do so. But do not keep me waiting too long."

He was silent for a moment and then he cried:

"Time is short. I cannot explain, but the sands of time are running out as far as I am concerned."

"What do you mean?" Cassandra asked.

"You would not understand," he answered, "but I can only beg you, Sandra, to let me grasp what little happiness I can. I need more desperately than I can explain the happiness of knowing you."

"You speak as . . . if you were . . . going away," Cassandra managed to say.

"That is in fact what will happen," the Duke said. "But until I do, I have to see you. I must see you!"

His arm drew her close. Then unexpectedly he released her and sat back in the corner of the cab.

"I sound almost hysterical," he said, "and I cannot explain."

"Why not?"

"Because, as you have just reminded me, we have only just met, because you do not wish me to kiss you, and because — how do I know that you are feeling as I am feeling tonight?"

"What . . . are you . . . feeling?"

"Do I have to answer that?" he asked. "I think you know that something entirely unusual has suddenly happened to me, and I am almost conceited enough to hope it has happened to you too."

He paused and then he said:

"Look at me, Sandra."

She turned her head and by the lights of the street lamp that were shining on both their faces, it was easy for her to see the expression in his eyes.

"You are so lovely," he said hoarsely, "so

incredibly, unbelievably lovely! Oh God! Why did I have to meet you at this particular moment of my life?"

The Duke called for Cassandra on the following morning at half past twelve.

She had begged him not to come earlier, knowing that it would take some time for her to explain to her Aunt that she was out to luncheon, get to the flat and change her clothes.

The most difficult person to deal with was Hannah who, having sat up until three o'clock the night before, was in a thoroughly disagreeable mood.

It had however not been such a hardship as she had tried to make out.

When Cassandra let herself into the flat, she had found Hannah fast asleep on a bed in the small bedroom, and it had been quite difficult to awaken her.

The Night-Porter had called them a cab, and they had driven back to Park Lane with Hannah not only grumbling every inch of the way but threatening to return to Yorkshire and tell Sir James what was going on.

Cassandra had managed to pacify her, but it had been difficult this morning to get her to return to the flat and help with her change of clothing.

The gown Cassandra was wearing when the Duke arrived was very attractive. At the same time it was a little too gaudy to be anything other than theatrical.

Of bronze silk trimmed with velvet, the skirt was draped at the front and swept behind into a bustle. The little jacket which ended at the waist was trimmed with fur and butoned down the front with imitation topazes.

Because she had real jewels to match, Cassandra could not resist wearing a topaz brooch, bracelet and ear-rings — a set which her father had given to her the previous year.

He had told her not to wear the ear-rings until she was married, but she thought now they made her look more sophisticated. They were also very fetching, with a bonnet trimmed with topaz-yellow feathers, which was tied under her chin with velvet ribbons.

Cassandra was only just ready and was waiting in the Sitting-room when the Duke knocked at the door of the flat.

She let him in and she could not disguise the amusement in her eyes as she watched him glance around at the over-decorated, vulgar Sitting-room.

"Is this yours?" he began with an incredulous note in his voice.

Then he exclaimed:

"But of course not! This is Hetty Henlow's flat! I have been here once before, many years ago."

"Then you know my landlady?" Cassandra laughed.

"I know old Lord Fitzmaurice who pays for it," the Duke replied. "He is a member of White's and he had been keeping Hetty for years!"

Cassandra stiffened.

She had never heard the expression before, but she could guess what it implied.

She suddenly felt ashamed that the Duke should see her in such a place.

Before, the flat had merely seemed common and gaudy, but now, being deeply in love, she could not bear him to associate her with anything crude or immoral.

"Let us go," she said quickly.

Without waiting for him to answer, she pulled open the door and started to descend the stairs.

Carrying his top hat and silver-headed cane, the Duke hurried after her.

When Cassandra reached Bury Street, she saw waiting outside a very smart Phaeton drawn by two horses.

"Are these yours?" she asked.

"About all I have left," he answered.

Once again she saw a cloud pass over his face.

"Surely you are not selling your carriage-horses or your hunters?" Cassandra said as she stepped into the Phaeton.

"Most of them have already gone," the Duke replied abruptly.

Cassandra had lain awake the best part of the night wondering exactly why the Duke wanted money so urgently.

Why, having written to her father, making it obvious that he was prepared to go on with the marriage as planned, was he now making what appeared to be an unnecessary sacrifice?

'I cannot understand it,' she had told herself again and again, and she thought the same now.

The Duke drove down Piccadilly with an expertise that she could not help admiring.

"You are looking very lovely," he said, as if forcing himself to change the subject. "I know that every man who sees us is filled with envy of me."

It was the sort of glib remark he would have made if she had in fact been an actress, and Cassandra resented it.

Then she realised that she was being very foolish.

She had set out to amuse and intrigue

him, so that she could learn the truth. And that was what she must continue to do.

She turned her face to look at him. With his top hat set at an angle on his dark hair, he looked slightly raffish and extremely handsome.

"Shall I tell you I am very honoured to be in such distinguished company, and with such an exceptionally attractive Duke?" she asked.

"Should I be flattered?" he asked. "Or suspicious that you have a hidden reason for being so kind to me?"

"Must I have a . . . reason?"

"No," he answered, "but I am half-afraid to put into your mind or mine the thoughts I really want you to think."

They were back again where they had been last night, Cassandra thought, fencing with words, hinting at what might or might not be below the surface.

She had the feeling that while they had been apart the Duke had thought about her as she had thought of him, but that he had decided that their relationship should be gay and amusing but by no means serious.

Accordingly she tried to play up to the mood he desired, but underneath everything they said, she felt there was a streak of seriousness which neither of them could ignore.

The Duke took her to 'The Café Royal' in Regent Street which was a popular place for luncheon and dinner.

It had not been open for many years but it had been a huge success from its very beginning. It was the first restaurant in London where an excellent and really French meal could be eaten.

Cassandra found it fascinating. It had atmosphere, and the big room with long, red, plush-covered seats contained a mixture of celebrities from all walks of life.

"Tell me who everybody is," she begged.

Amused by her interest and curiosity, the Duke pointed out the actors, crooks, jockeys, confidence-men, trainers, owners and professional backers who were all eating the superlative food and drinking wine from a cellar which was acknowledged to be one of the best in London.

When Oscar Wilde came in looking pale, elegant and extremely pleased with himself, Cassandra exclaimed excitedly:

"I have always wanted to see him. I have enjoyed his poems so much. But my father has always said he is a terrible *poseur*."

"He is," the Duke answered. "Nevertheless he undoubtedly has great talent."

There were of course a number of women in the Restaurant who were either actresses or quite obviously of a class with which Cassandra had never come in contact.

However, after her initial interest in the other guests, she found it difficult to notice anyone but the Duke.

Once again, she found it easy to talk to him, to discuss so many different subjects.

It seemed they could hardly pause for breath before they were arguing, discussing, exclaiming over something else!

When finally they drove away in the direction of Knightsbridge Green, Cassandra's eyes were shining and she was feeling as happy as she had felt the night before. Never had she enjoyed a meal more.

She had been to Tattersall's with her father on a Sunday some years previously, and she remembered the great grass-covered yard where the horses were shown off to prospective buyers.

She knew there were seventy-five open boxes and twenty-five stables for brood mares, above which there was a Gallery served by lifts for storing carriages and harness.

When she had been there before, the yard had been filled with top-hatted gentlemen and elegantly-dressed ladies, while grooms had trotted the horses up to the Auctioneer's box and back.

Today there were only the grooms in their shirt sleeves, moving amongst the stalls, carrying buckets of water, whistling through their teeth as they rubbed down their charges.

For the first time Cassandra saw the Duke in a very different guise. It was almost as if he had forgotten her very existence.

His head-groom reported to him on the way in which the horses had travelled, telling him that one was nervous after the journey, another seemed a little off-colour, but the majority were settling into their new quarters.

"Keep them as quiet as you can," the Duke said.

"I'm seeing to that, Your Grace! A nervous horse never gets the best price."

"That is very true."

The Duke then went with Cassandra to look at the horses, one after another. There was no doubt they were magnificent animals.

"I have put a reserve of one thousand guineas on this one," the Duke said. "He has already won three races and seems sure to win the Gold Cup at Ascot."

"Would you not be wise to keep him then?" Cassandra asked, knowing the Gold Cup brought in a large amount of prize money.

"I cannot afford to wait," the Duke answered and went on to the next stall.

Cassandra asked for a catalogue of the sale on Monday.

A member of the Tattersall's staff brought it to her, and she looked through it wondering as she did so, if her father had seen a copy.

Almost as if he read her thoughts the Duke said:

"I only decided to put my horses in the sale a week ago. You will therefore find they have been added at the last moment and listed all together at the end of the catalogue."

"But surely that means that the addition has not gone to many of the people in the country who receive it regularly before every sale," Cassandra said.

The Duke shrugged his shoulders.

"Perhaps. But I am sure there will be no lack of bidders. My father's Stud is well known in racing circles."

"Yes, of course," Cassandra answered.

She was however thinking that Sir James being in Yorkshire could not have heard that the Duke's horses were in this sale.

If he had, she was quite certain he would have mentioned it to her. This meant that there was not time for her to communicate with him, unless she sent him a telegram.

If she did that, she argued to herself, he would undoubtedly come to London, in which case she could no longer go on acting her part of a young unknown actress.

Besides, if Sir James was in London, there was every likelihood that he would introduce her to the Duke. It would be so easy for it to happen, even if she did not go with him to the sale.

An idea came to her. When they left Tattersall's she took the sale catalogue carefully with her and sat with it on her lap in the Phaeton so that she would not forget it.

"You are dining with me tonight," the Duke said.

It was a statement rather than a question.

"If you still want me to do so," Cassandra answered. "Are you quite certain you have not had enough of my company?"

"You are fishing for compliments," the Duke replied with a smile.

He looked at her and added:

"You know I want to be with you — to see you. Do not play with me, Sandra. I cannot bear it."

There was something almost desperate in his voice, and again Cassandra did not know what was happening.

She only felt that she was being carried

along on a tide which was moving too quickly for her to have any clear or coherent thoughts about herself or her relationship with the Duke.

She knew only that he overwhelmed her, that it was a joy beyond words to be with him, to know that he was beside her, to listen to his voice speaking to her and to see his eyes looking into hers.

And because she felt it was all too wonderful to put into words or even to contemplate, it was dangerous.

Dangerous because she might forget that it was only a performance, that their relationship had no substance, no foundation in reality.

She was an actress he found pretty and attractive, and he was a Duke who was about to become engaged to a rich heiress.

Cassandra felt as if she had embarked in a journey the end of which she could not foresee.

Her plan of meeting the Duke, of finding out the truth about his interests, and most of all whom he was in love with, appeared to be going well.

Yet there were so many new depths to it, so many hazards and difficulties which she had not anticipated.

The whole idea had been, she thought, a

fairy story that she had told herself.

She had imagined it for so many years that to put it into operation had been easy.

Yet now she was afraid, uncertain of what might happen next.

She only knew there was in her an uneasiness, a kind of growing fear that lay beneath the excitement and the sheer delight of being with the Duke.

Of knowing too that she loved him more every minute they were together.

Cassandra was ready a quarter of an hour before the Duke called for her at Bury Street.

Because she could not bear him to see her again in the garish Sitting-room which belonged to Hetty Henlow, she watched from a window until she saw the carriage arrive.

Then she ran downstairs.

She met him in the Hall and he raised her hand to his lips.

"I have not kept you waiting?" he asked in surprise.

"No, but I thought I would save you climbing two flights," Cassandra answered.

"You are very considerate."

She was wearing tonight a white gown which, like the one she had worn the previous night, sparkled with sequins and was ornamented with bunches of artificial flowers.

It was elaborate, beautiful and theatrical.

Hannah had set two white roses in her hair and tonight Cassandra discarded her earrings and wore instead a two-string pearl necklace which belonged to her mother.

It was very valuable and she hoped the Duke would think the pearls were artificial, but when she saw him notice them while they were having dinner, she realised he was not deceived.

He took her to dine at Rule's, a much quieter place than Romano's.

It was small and intimate and the other diners were mostly, like themselves, couples who were intensely interested in each other and who wanted to talk in low voices.

"If it seems dull, there will be many more people here after the theatres close," the Duke apologized.

"I am very content with it as it is," Cassandra answered.

"That is what I hoped you would say."

They sat talking over their meal, and afterwards Cassandra found it difficult to remember what they had discussed.

She only knew that the Duke not only made her quiver when his hand touched hers, but he stimulated her mind so that her brain responded to his and everything they said seemed to have a special meaning.

"I have never known a Sandra before," he said to her one moment during dinner. "I suppose it is a diminutive of Alexandra?"

Cassandra parried the question by saying:

"I hope Your Grace lives up to your name?"

"What do you know about it?" the Duke asked with a smile.

"I know that Marcus Terentius Varro was the greatest scholar of the Roman Republic. He is said to have written more than six hundred books on a wide range of subjects."

"Where did you look that up?" the Duke enquired. "The British Museum?"

"You know as well as I do that I have had no time to visit Museums since I arrived in London," Cassandra answered, "but I find the name rather fascinating."

"And what about its owner?" the Duke enquired.

His eyes looked down into hers and once again she knew he was searching for something. Because his scrutiny made her feel shy, she looked away from him.

"What are you thinking?" he asked in a low voice.

"I am thinking about you."

"And what conclusions have you reached?"

"Perhaps I was . . . trying to read your . . . thoughts."

"Can you do that?"

"Sometimes."

"Then tell me what I am thinking."

"You are worrying," Cassandra answered. "I think that you are standing, one might say, at a cross-roads in your life. You have made a decision and you are not certain if it is the right one."

The Duke stared at her in astonishment.

"How could you know that?"

"Is it true?"

"Yes, it is true. But what you have not seen, is the reason why I am worried."

"Will you tell me what it is?"

"That is not difficult — it is you!"

She turned to look at him and again his eyes held hers so that she felt something quiver within her and come to life. For a moment they were both spellbound.

Then, as they looked at each other quite oblivious of their surroundings, a voice said:

"What a pleasant surprise to find you both here!"

Cassandra looked up to see Lord Carwen standing by their table.

"Good-evening, Sandra," he said and held out his hand.

She did not wish to touch him but she

179

could not help but put her hand in his.

He kissed her fingers lightly, then he put his other hand on the Duke's shoulder as he would have risen.

"Do not get up, dear boy," he said. "I have just written to you, as it happens and sent my letter round to White's."

"Is it anything of importance?" the Duke enquired.

Cassandra thought there was a worried note in his voice.

"No, it is only an invitation to ask you to stay tomorrow until Monday. Lily will be coming after the theatre tomorrow evening, and there will be various other mutual friends whom you should find amusing."

"It is very kind of you," the Duke began, "but . . ."

"Of course," Lord Carwen interrupted, "the invitation includes the beautiful Miss Sandra Standish."

He smiled at Cassandra in a manner which was somehow distasteful.

"I would, pretty little lady, have written to you direct," he went on, "but you omitted to say good-night to me last night, and so unfortunately I was unable to ask for your address."

"I am sorry if I seemed . . . rude," Cassandra murmured.

"I missed you," Lord Carwen said, "and

so to assuage my disappointment at not being able to dance with you again, will you come with Varro and stay at my house in the country?"

Cassandra was about to refuse.

Then the thought came to her how wonderful it would be to drive into the country with the Duke.

They would be together and be able to see more of each other than was possible just by meeting for meals.

As she hesitated, Lord Carwen said to the Duke, with an insistent note in his voice:

"You must come, Varro. I will not take 'No' for an answer!"

"Then we have no choice," the Duke said. "That is, if Sandra will agree."

"I cannot believe that Sandra would be so hard-hearted as to cast me into the depths of despair by refusing my hospitality," Lord Carwen said.

He picked up Cassandra's hand as he spoke and kissed her fingers again.

"I must go back to my party, but I shall expect you both about tea-time tomorrow. Varro will doubtless explain what clothes you will find necessary. I promise you a very entertaining time!"

"Thank you," Cassandra said in a small voice.

As Lord Carwen walked away, she felt he had cast a shadow over their evening.

Although they stayed for another hour or so, Cassandra was aware of him all the time. He was the other side of the room surrounded by his friends, yet she felt as if he was eavesdropping at their table.

As if he felt the same, the Duke asked for the bill.

"Do you want to go and stay with him?" he asked.

They both knew to whom he was referring without his mentioning a name.

"No," Cassandra answered, "but I would like to be in the country with you."

"Then we will go," the Duke said decisively, as if there had been a question in his mind about refusing the invitation.

Cassandra had the strange feeling that he was in some way compelled to do what Lord Carwen wished.

Because she wanted to make things easier for him she said:

"It will be nice to see Mrs. Langtry again. Do you think Mr. Gebhard will come with her?"

"But of course," the Duke replied, "you do not imagine that she would go anywhere without him?"

Cassandra had not thought that it would

be possible for a married woman to take another man with her to stay in a country house as if he were her husband.

Then she told herself there were special rules for actresses.

Nevertheless Mrs. Langtry was a lady, and she wondered what her mother would have thought of such behavior.

The Duke having paid the bill rose and Cassandra preceded him across the room.

So many people had arrived since they had come in that she thought they might have difficulty in finding the velvet wrap that matched her white dress.

Rather than sending a waiter for it, she herself went to the cloak-room.

There were dozens of wraps, cloaks and coats in the charge of a woman wearing a black dress and a white, frilled apron.

"I'm not quite certain which is yours, Madam," she said apologetically.

Cassandra was helping her find it when there was a little sound behind her. She turned to see a young woman who had just entered the cloak-room collapse slowly onto the floor.

She hurried to her and recognised that she was one of the guests in Lord Carwen's party.

With the help of the cloak-room attendant Cassandra assisted her to a couch.

"I think the lady has fainted," she said.

"I'll get some brandy, Ma'am," the attendant murmured and hurried away.

Cassandra rubbed the woman's hands which were very cold and after a moment her eyes fluttered open.

She was pretty in a rather obvious manner, with very fair hair and gold-specked hazel eyes which held a frightened look.

But Cassandra thought that, unlike Connie Gilchrist, she was obviously well-bred and a lady.

"It is all right," she said. "You have only fainted. Lie still."

At that moment the cloak-room attendant came back with a small glass of brandy and Cassandra persuaded the girl to take a few sips.

The spirit brought the colour back into her cheeks, and after a moment she took the glass from Cassandra's hand and drank a little more.

"It was . . . stupid of me," she said, "but I have been feeling . . . ill all the evening."

"Perhaps you had better go home," Cassandra suggested. "Is there anyone of your party who will escort you?"

"No, no-one. Lord Carwen invited me to supper last night when I was at his party, and his carriage was waiting for me after the theatre."

"Shall I send him a message?" Cassandra asked.

"No! No! I do not want to worry him. I do not know him well. He was just filling up the party which he was giving for Sylvia Grey, who is in the cast."

Cassandra realised she had not recognised the Gaiety star in Lord Carwen's party, but then she had not looked at them very closely.

"Well, perhaps my friend and I could take you home," Cassandra said doubtfully. "Do you live far away?"

"No. It is quite a short distance behind Drury Lane."

"Then that would be the best solution," Cassandra said. "Are you sure we should not inform Lord Carwen that you are ill?"

"No! All I want to do is go home to bed and lie down. I should not have come. I found it difficult enough to get through the performance."

"It must have been very hard, feeling as you do," Cassandra said sympathetically.

Still very pale, her hands shaking a little, the young woman rose to her feet.

"Are you quite sure," she asked as the cloak-room attendant brought her wrap, "that you do not mind taking me home? I can easily go alone."

"You are not well enough," Cassandra answered, "you might faint again."

"I think — I am all right."

"Then come along," Cassandra smiled. "The sooner you are in bed the better. What is your name, by the way?"

"My name is Nancy — Nancy Wood."

"Then if you are certain you do not wish to say good-bye to Lord Carwen, we will leave a message with the Head Waiter."

Cassandra was sure it was best to take the young actress away. She looked so ill that she would be a damper on the gaiety of any party.

Putting an arm around her to support her, she helped her outside to where the Duke was waiting. He looked surprised as they appeared.

"This is Miss Nancy Wood," Cassandra said. "She is performing at the Gaiety and you may have seen her. She is feeling very ill and I said we would take her home."

"But of course," the Duke replied.

It was nice of him, Cassandra thought, not to ask questions, not to fuss, but to assist Nancy Wood out through the door and into the carriage.

She sat back in a corner and closed her eyes.

Cassandra sat down beside her and the Duke seated himself opposite them.

Nancy gave her address in a far away voice which made Cassandra think she might faint again at any moment.

They drove in silence and, as Nancy Wood had said, it was not far to go.

The streets at the back of Drury Lane were narrow, squalid and dirty. The house at which they stopped was certainly far from prepossessing.

"Have you a key?" the Duke asked.

With some difficulty Nancy Wood found it in her reticule.

The Duke opened the door and with Cassandra's assistance they got the sick woman out of the carriage and onto the pavement.

"I had better take her inside," Cassandra said in a low voice.

"Can you manage?" he asked.

She smiled at him.

"I am sure I can."

She put her arm around Nancy Wood and took her inside the house which had a straight staircase running up almost perpendicular to the first floor.

The place smelt of dirt, gas and cooking. As they laboriously climbed the staircase, Cassandra could not help thinking how squalid it was.

The stairs could not have been scrubbed for years and the linoleum which covered them was full of holes.

Nancy Wood had another key which opened the door of a back room. She lit a candle which revealed an unmade bed and a terrible state of untidiness.

There were clothes hanging on the outside of a broken wardrobe. There were stockings, underclothes, petticoats and gowns thrown on a chair and also on the bed.

Shoes were scattered along the side of the wall and the dressing-table was littered with paraphernalia of every sort.

There were hair-brushes that needed washing, combs without teeth, grease-paint, mascara and artificial flowers which looked as if they should have been thrown away years ago.

"It is in rather a mess," Nancy Wood said weakly.

"Never mind about it now," Cassandra answered. "Get into bed. You will feel better in the morning, and if not, you must see a doctor."

"There is . . . nothing a doctor can do for . . . me," Nancy said.

She sat down on the crumpled bed and her whole body seemed to sag dejectedly.

"Why? What is wrong with you?" Cassandra asked.

"I'm having a baby," Nancy Wood answered and burst into tears.

Chapter Six

Cassandra came down the steep stairs and saw the Duke waiting for her below.

He looked up at her with a worried expression on his face.

"You have been a long time."

"She is . . . ill," Cassandra answered, "and I do not . . . know what to . . . do."

She spoke hesitatingly. When she reached his side he asked:

"What is wrong with her?"

Cassandra did not answer. Then, as she realised he was waiting, she said uncomfortably, a blush deepening the colour in her cheeks:

"I . . . cannot . . . tell you."

"I suppose she is having a baby?"

The Duke's words brought the color flooding into her face and her eyes widened as she exclaimed in surprise:

"How did you . . . guess?"

"There is nothing you can do," he said sharply.

"But she is so . . . distressed."

The Duke seemed to consider for a moment. Then he said:

"Did you leave her any money?"

"I did not think of it," Cassandra replied.

"Wait here!"

He started up the staircase.

"No! you cannot go to her!" Cassandra cried. "She is . . . in bed."

The Duke appeared not to have heard her. Before she could say any more, he had reached the landing, and she heard him knock at Nancy Wood's door and walk in.

Cassandra waited irresolutely, not sure what she should do.

She was shocked at the idea of the Duke going into the untidy, squalid room where she had helped Nancy into bed, but she was much more shocked at having spoken to him of her having a baby.

No lady would have thought of saying anything so intimate to a man.

Even with her contemporaries, a married woman would only talk of being in an "interesting condition" or of "expecting an addition to the family."

To discuss such personal matters with anyone but her mother or her husband, was to be incredibly coarse and crude.

The actual arrival of a child into the world was to Cassandra, as to average young women of her age, wrapped in as deep a mystery as the manner in which it was conceived.

The fact that Nancy Wood had blurted out her condition had struck her with almost the same effect as a bombshell!

She did not know what to say! While Nancy wept bitterly, she could only offer some practical assistance in helping her to undress and mutter words of consolation which even to her own ears sounded ineffective.

It seemed incredible to Cassandra that the Duke should have guessed so quickly what was wrong, and when in a few minutes he came down the stairs, she found it hard to meet his eyes.

He did not speak. He merely took her by the arm, opened the front door, and when they were outside assisted her into the carriage.

He gave Cassandra's address to the Coachman and the horses set off at a good pace, since the streets, although narrow, were at this hour of the evening empty of pedestrians.

"I did not think of giving her . . . money," Cassandra said after a moment. "It was stupid of me, but in any case I had none with me."

"There is nothing else you can do," the Duke said firmly.

"I must try to help her," Cassandra argued. "She cannot go back to her family."

"Why not?"

"Because she ran away from home to go on the stage. Her father, who is a Parson, is Vicar of a Parish in Wiltshire. She has not communicated with him since she came to London."

"There is nowhere else for her to go," the Duke said in what Cassandra thought was a hard voice.

"There must be . . . somewhere," she answered desperately.

"You cannot entangle yourself with this chorus girl. You never saw her before tonight, and it is just unfortunate that you should have happened to be there when she fainted."

"I think you are being hard-hearted, and perhaps rather cruel," Cassandra said. "She is in trouble and someone has to help her."

"I have left her some money," the Duke replied, "and I will take her more tomorrow."

"That is very kind of you," Cassandra said, her voice softening. "When she can no longer . . . act, she will have to live somewhere. I doubt whether, even if she wished to keep her . . . baby in that terrible little room, the Landlord would permit it."

The Duke was silent and after a moment Cassandra said:

"I thought that the . . . father of the child would help her. But she said . . . something I did not understand."

"What was that?"

"She said she did not . . . know who he . . . was! How could it be . . . possible that she does not . . . know?"

The Duke did not reply.

He turned to look at Cassandra's profile in the light from the street lamps. Her straight little nose was etched against the darkness of the carriage, as was the soft curve of her lips and the firm line of her chin.

"How old are you?" he asked unexpectedly.

Cassandra thought he was deliberately changing the subject, and she did not know what to reply.

To say she was only twenty would, she thought, make her seem too young to have played many parts on the stage. On the other hand she felt a strong reluctance to lie to the Duke.

She had already told him so many falsehoods, and she wished now she could be frank and that there were no secrets between them.

"I have always been told," she answered at length, in what she hoped was a light tone but which sounded very immature, "that it is extremely . . . rude to ask a lady . . . her age."

"You must accept my apologies," the Duke said.

They drove on in silence and it was not long before they reached Bury Street. The footman on the box of the carriage alighted to arouse the night-porter.

As they waited for the man to open the door the Duke said:

"Try not to worry, Sandra. I will call for you tomorrow at twelve o'clock and, if it pleases you, we will go to see this woman before we proceed to the country."

"I would like to do that," Cassandra said. "Thank you."

The night-porter had opened the door and Cassandra put her hands down to lift her skirt so that she could step out on to the pavement.

"You will be all right?" the Duke asked. "I do not like to think of you alone in that flat."

"I am not alone," Cassandra answered without thinking.

She did not notice that he stiffened, nor did she see the strange expression on his face.

Cassandra was ready just before twelve noon the following morning, but it had been a tremendous effort.

First of all she had had to explain to her

Aunt that she was going away until Monday. Lady Fladbury was curious.

"Who are these friends with whom you will be staying?" she enquired.

Cassandra thought it best to tell the truth.

"I have been invited to Lord Carwen's house, which is only about three-quarters of an hour out of London."

"The Carwens'?" Lady Fladbury exclaimed. "I thought Her Ladyship was seldom in England. She prefers Paris, being half-French. I have never met her, but I heard she is a beautiful woman and Lord Carwen has the reputation of being extremely gay."

"He is quite old," Cassandra said, thinking that made it sound more respectable.

"He is only about forty!" Lady Fladbury retorted. "Of course that seems old to you, but I dare say there will be a number of young people in the house-party. Enjoy yourself, my dear!"

"I am sure I shall," Cassandra answered, feeling she had jumped the first fence.

Hannah had been far more difficult.

"If you're staying in a decent house, Miss Cassandra, why aren't you taking me?" she demanded angrily. "You know as well as I do that where you have been invited before it has always been understood that you bring your Lady's-maid."

"Yes, I know, Hannah," Cassandra answered, "but this is a large house-party and I think they find visiting maids a nuisance."

"I don't know what your mother would say, I don't really! Going off alone like this!" Hannah said. "And if it's all above-board and respectable why can't His Lordship fetch you from here?"

"Please, Hannah, help me," Cassandra pleaded. "I told you I was acting a part, and I promise you there is nothing wrong in the place where I am going. Aunt Eleanor knows all about Lord and Lady Carwen, and if there was anything wrong she would have told me about it."

"Well, I don't like it and that's a fact!" Hannah said positively. "While I'm able to keep my eye on you, I know you can't get into any real mischief, but to stay in a strange place without me — Heaven knows what might happen!"

"What could happen?" Cassandra asked. "And it is only for two nights. Come to the flat on Monday morning and wait for me. If I am not there before luncheon, I shall certainly arrive soon afterwards."

Grumbling, muttering to herself, and being extremely disagreeable, Hannah began to pack the clothes she thought Cassandra would require.

Then they took the trunks to the flat in Bury Street and she packed Cassandra's theatrical clothes under protest.

On one thing Hannah was adamant and made such a scene that Cassandra was obliged to give in to her.

She insisted that Cassandra should travel to the country in one of her own gowns covered with a cloak which was both warm and decorative.

"You'll catch your death of cold in these new flimsy garments in which no respectable young woman would be seen," Hannah said aggressively. "Besides, you'll look a figure of fun arriving to stay at a country house in something that's only fit to be worn on the other side of the footlights."

Finally, because it was too exhausting to argue further, Cassandra gave in and wore the gown of sapphire blue velvet which had cost her father a large sum at Jay's.

It had a velvet bonnet in the same colour trimmed demurely only with little bows of ribbon.

It made her look very young, but it also threw into prominence the dazzling whiteness of her skin and accentuated the gold lights in her red hair.

Cassandra remembered consolingly that people thought she looked theatrical without the addition of the gowns she had bought at Chasemore's. She doubted if the Duke would notice any appreciable difference from her appearance on the previous day.

Besides the difficulties of getting ready, moving her trunks to Bury Street, and keeping Hannah from open rebellion, she had a very special letter to write.

Once again she forged her father's handwriting on the engraved writing-paper she had brought from Yorkshire, as she wrote to Tattersall's Salesroom instructing them to buy all the Duke's horses when they came up for sale on Monday.

As she signed her father's signature, Cassandra knew that this action put a time limit on the length of her stay in London.

She would have to arrive home before he received a notification from Tattersall's of their purchases for him together with the bill for them.

She was quite certain in her own mind that she was only anticipating her father's wishes in buying the Duke's horses; but at the same time she was well aware she would have some explaining to do, and that she would have to do it in person.

Even to herself, she would not face up to what she expected to happen between today and Tuesday morning when she must go back to Yorkshire.

Once again she was conscious of being swept along on a flowing tide. Once again she was aware that something tremendous was happening, but she could not formulate it to herself.

She only knew that she loved the Duke overwhelmingly.

Every hour she was away from him seemed to pass so slowly that it might have been a year, a century. But when she was with him, time flashed by so that the moment of parting seemed always to be upon them.

He had said that for him "the sands were running out", and Cassandra felt the same expression was true for herself — and yet what did she hope or fear for the future?

She dispatched a footman from Park Lane to Tattersall's Salesrooms before she travelled to the flat in a closed carriage with Hannah.

"I can't imagine what the Coachman'll be thinking of us going to such a place," Hannah said sourly.

"I hope you told the servants that I had a friend I visited in Bury Street."

"I'm not soiling my mouth with a lot of

lies, Miss Cassandra," Hannah said tartly, "and I've always believed 'least said, soonest mended'."

It was true that Hannah was not a gossip, Cassandra thought, but she too had taken a violent dislike to the flat and she knew she would be extremely glad when she could see the last of it.

She left all her trunks but one in the Hall. The porter carried up only the round topped piece in which she wished Hannah to pack the gowns from Chasemore's.

Hannah sniffed and muttered all the time she was folding them, and just as she finished, Cassandra, who had been watching from the window, exclaimed:

"The carriage is here! Oh! I think there are two of them."

She had not told Hannah who was fetching her, and now she hurried down the stairs to greet the Duke as he stepped into the hall.

"I am ready," she said with a lilt of joy in her voice.

She saw that his eyes rested on her admiringly and was glad that after all she had conceded a victory to Hannah by wearing the sapphire outfit.

"I see you have a warm cloak," he said. "I am glad about that, because as it is a fine day I suggest that we drive in my open Phaeton. If it rains there is a hood we can raise. I have also brought a brake for our luggage. My valet will see to yours."

"I shall enjoy being in the fresh air," Cassandra replied.

She noticed that today the Duke had a different Phaeton from the one he had used the day before, when there had been a groom seated behind them.

Built for speed, there was room for only two people in it.

She saw a man climb down from the brake which was driven by a Coachman wearing the Alchester livery and a cockaded tall hat.

She thought, as she saw him enter the flat that she had been wise to tell Hannah to put the trunk that had been packed upstairs outside on the landing and close the door.

She did not want Hannah to meet the Duke's servants.

The Duke helped her into the phaeton, and as they set off down Jermyn Street, Cassandra said:

"You have not forgotten that we are going to see Nancy?"

"I have already been there."

"You have," Cassandra ejaculated in surprise. "How was she?"

In reply the Duke held out an envelope

which she took from him. There was a grim expression on his face which made her exclaim:

"What has happened? What did she say?"

"She was not there," the Duke said quietly.

Cassandra stared at him in surprise then she looked at the envelope he had given her.

Written on the outside was just her name: "Sandra".

She opened it. Inside was a brief letter written in an educated, tidy handwriting, but in pencil.

"You were so kind, but there is nothing you or anyone else can do for me. I would rather face God than my father! He is more likely to forgive me.
                    Nancy."

Cassandra read it through. Then she said fearfully:

"What does she mean? Where had she gone? I do not . . . understand."

"I went up to her bed-room," the Duke answered. "The door was unlocked and she was not there. On the dressing-table I found this letter and the money I had given to her last night."

"But what had she . . . done?" Cassandra cried.

"I think it is obvious," the Duke answered, "that she has taken the easiest way out of her dilemma. She really had little alternative."

"You mean she has . . . killed herself?"

"I imagine she will be one of the unidentified bodies that are fished out of the river every day," the Duke said. "Many of them are in the same condition as Nancy Wood."

"But we must do something . . . find out for certain."

"It would involve you with the police," the Duke said, "and I do not think that is at all desirable."

At the thought of the police Cassandra was suddenly still.

"After all," the Duke went on, "all we have to show them is this note left for you. We do not know how to find her father, his name may not even be Wood."

"No . . . of course . . . not," Cassandra agreed.

"It would cause a scandal for you and for me to be involved publicly in this tragedy," the Duke continued. "And we are too late to help her."

"But will not the . . . police, or Nancy's landlord make inquiries?"

"I doubt if either of them will trouble themselves unduly," the Duke replied.

"The police will find it difficult to discover who she is. The landlord, when she does not return, will pocket the money which we left behind in lieu of rent and dispose of her belongings."

Cassandra sat stunned by shock. At the same time she knew that if the police discovered that she and the Duke were the last people to see Nancy alive, her subterfuge would be revealed.

Her father would be furious if this happened, and she was well aware what a story the newspapers would make of it.

But she was at the moment very appalled at the thought of what had happened to Nancy.

"It is horrible! It is cruel! How could she have . . . done such a . . . thing?" Cassandra cried.

The Duke did not reply but concentrated on driving his horses. After a moment she went on in a low voice:

"She told me last night that her father would never . . . forgive her. It seems . . . un-Christian and . . . wicked to punish her so . . . severely."

The Duke still made no answer. Cassandra stared ahead seeing only Nancy Wood's white, frightened face, hearing the despairing note in her voice which had been followed by a flood of hopeless tears.

After they had driven for some distance, the Duke said:

"I want you to try to forget what has happened. It is something that you should not have experienced. Dwelling on it will help no-one."

He paused as if he searched for words before he continued:

"I cannot help thinking that from her own point of view Nancy Wood did the best thing possible. What future could there possibly be for her or her child?"

That was a sensible view, Cassandra had to agree, and yet she could only feel almost physically sick at the thought of the wretched girl going out, perhaps at dawn, to seek oblivion in the dark cold waters of the Thames.

But she told herself that the Duke was right.

To keep thinking about it, to wonder if she could have prevented such a tragedy, to reproach herself for not having given Nancy Wood more help than she had been able to do, would only make her miserable to no purpose and would ruin this lovely day alone with the Duke.

She could quite understand that he found this whole subject distasteful, but in a way, she wished she could have asked him more questions.

She wanted to understand how a Vicar's daughter, brought up in a decent household, could have got herself into such trouble, and why there was no man to marry her, thereby making the child legitimate.

There were so many questions to which Cassandra could not find an answer, but she knew that she must not pester the Duke with them.

In any case in all probability he would refuse to reply.

It all seemed to her very mysterious, but at the same time, she had only to think of the dirty boarding-house and Nancy Wood's untidy, squalid bed-room to see that for his sake she must try to forget.

With an effort, Cassandra told herself to think of the Duke. He wanted to be amused, to be gay. This situation could do nothing but irritate and embarrass him.

She could almost feel it putting a barrier between them.

So, desperately, because she felt her own happiness slipping away from her, Cassandra tried to talk of other things.

As if he understood the effort she was making, the Duke talked of his horses.

He told Cassandra the pedigrees of the ones he was driving, described some of the sales he had visited in his father's time.

The old Duke had gloried in visiting Horse-fairs all over the country, always hoping, as many owners had hoped, before him, to discover a Derby winner being sold for a few pounds.

"Some men collect horses, as other men collect pictures and 'objets d'art'," the Duke smiled.

"Is that what you would like to do?"

"I have no opportunity of doing either at the moment," he replied. "If I had the chance, I would be greedy and collect both!"

"I am sure you have some very fine pictures at Alchester Park," Cassandra said.

"The family collection is unique," he said. "Every head of the family and his wife all down the ages have been painted for posterity — some by great artists — some by what my father used to call 'the Village carpenter'."

He laughed.

"But they are all there, first the Earls and Countesses of Alchester, and — then after the Dukedom was created, every Duke and Duchess."

"Has your portrait yet been added to the others?" Cassandra asked.

"No," the Duke replied. "It is traditional that the owner of the title waits until he is married."

As he spoke Cassandra saw a shadow cross his face.

She knew he was thinking of the marriage that had been arranged for him years ago and to which today he was committing himself.

She had an impulse to tell him the truth — and then quite suddenly she was afraid.

When she had planned this wild escapade, she had known that at the back of her mind lay the idea that if after all the Duke was not in love with someone else she might be able to attract him.

Then as in a fairy story, she would only have to throw off her disguise and reveal her true identity.

Now for the first time she had the feeling that the Duke might well resent being tricked and imposed upon.

Her dreams had all been concerned with what was really a card-board figure of a man. The pictures and portraits of the Marquis had filled her adolescent dreams.

But they were not of a man who was flesh and blood; a man who had kissed the palm of her hand and wished to kiss her lips; a man who had said that only actors and actresses were free to be themselves.

'I have made a mess of it!' Cassandra admitted to herself frankly.

And her brain was busy with how she could extricate herself from a position that she felt now might so easily be misinterpreted.

They had been driving in to the country for some time before Cassandra asked where they were going.

"Lord Carwen's house is only three-quarters of an hour's drive from London, I thought," she said. "Surely we shall arrive too soon? He did not ask us until tea-time."

"I have no intention of turning up one moment before we have to," the Duke answered. "I am taking you to luncheon at an Inn which I think you will enjoy. It is on the river and later in the year is very popular, but I do not think today we will find it very crowded."

The Duke was right in his assumption. The Inn was charming.

Having arranged stabling for the horses, he escorted Cassandra to the Dining-room and they were seated at a table in the window, overlooking the slow moving silver Thames.

The Inn was old, with great oak beams and a huge open fireplace in which a log-fire was burning.

The Duke ordered wine and the meal, though simple, was well-cooked and palatable.

It was easy as they faced each other across the small table in the window to forget the tragedy of Nancy Wood and to pick up their discussion where they had left off the night before.

Cassandra realised she had been right in thinking that the Duke was extremely clever.

She knew that she herself had an intelligence superior to many of her contemporaries.

There was no doubt that they stimulated each other's mind, capped each other's quotations, and were able to argue as equals.

"How dare you be beautiful as well as clever?" the Duke demanded at one moment when he found some argument of Cassandra's unanswerable.

"You do not make that sound as if it were a compliment," Cassandra replied.

"It is not!" the Duke said. "Most men dislike clever women. They are frightened of them."

"And you?"

"I find you very interesting, Sandra, but it perplexes me why, being so intelligent, you have chosen your particular profession."

"There are not many careers open to women," Cassandra replied.

"That is true," the Duke answered. "Who would want to see women Members of Parliament, women lawyers, women stockbrokers, or worst of all — a woman Judge!"

"Why would that be so horrifying?" Cassandra asked.

"Because women are always prejudiced. Their minds are supremely illogical."

This was a provocation Cassandra could not let pass, and once again they were arguing fiercely with each other, until the Duke threw himself back in his seat to say:

"I take back all I said! You are a bluestocking! If you were my daughter I should pack you off to Oxford and see how you fared at Somerville amongst the student feminists."

Cassandra smiled and he added:

"You see, it is really not fair when you look like that with your lips curved in a smile. No man could refuse you anything, whatever the odds against him!"

They sat for a long time after luncheon was over.

There had been few other guests in the Inn besides themselves, and when they had departed the waiters seemed to disappear too, and Cassandra and the Duke were alone.

"I wish we did not have to leave here to go

on to this boring house-party," he said suddenly.

"Will it be boring?" Cassandra enquired.

"There will be other people there," he replied, "and I want you to myself. I want to talk to you; to listen to you; to be with you. Anyone else, whoever they may be, will be an interruption which I shall resent."

"I, too, would . . . much rather be just with . . . you," Cassandra murmured.

"Do you mean that?" he asked.

He leaned forward as he spoke and took her hand in his.

Once again she felt herself quiver because he was touching her. As their eyes met, he said in a low voice:

"Do you know what has happened to us, Sandra?"

She did not reply and after a moment he went on:

"I think I fell in love with you the moment we were introduced. It was not only that I thought you more lovely and attractive than anyone I had ever seen before, but there was something else. Did you feel it too?"

It was impossible for Cassandra to speak, her heart was thumping so wildly in her breast. Then the Duke released her hand and stood up.

"There is no point in talking about it," he

said harshly. "Come! If I take you by a somewhat roundabout route so that you can see the countryside we should arrive at exactly the right time at His Lordship's residence."

For a moment it was difficult for Cassandra to move.

She felt as if by his abruptness he had slapped her in the face. Then suddenly she realised she faced a new and even worse dilemma.

The Duke had admitted loving her, but he was not prepared to do anything about it!

His head would rule his heart! Money was more important to him than love!

Because Cassandra loved him so that her whole being vibrated with it, she could not bear the thought that his love for her was something he could set aside for mercenary reasons.

Now she knew that she had brought upon herself an agony that was almost impossible to contemplate.

He loved her!

He had fallen in love with her just as she had hoped he would, but he was quite prepared to give her up for a rich heiress he had never seen, but who would bring him the millions he needed.

It had been bad enough to envisage the

Duke, her ideal man, the hero of her girlish dreams, being in love with someone else.

But that he should be in love with her, and yet not have the courage to do anything about it, was a pain beyond anything she had imagined she might endure.

As she rose from her seat at the table, she felt as if she could not go on with the farce any longer.

Then she knew that having once embarked on this crazy adventure, she must continue playing her assumed part at least until they returned to London.

She could not face him now with the truth!

She could not bear either the contempt with which he might treat her or worse still, his delight in finding that he could have from the asking both the woman he loved and the money which he needed so desperately!

'I cannot bear it,' Cassandra whispered to herself.

She knew that if she had thought it difficult to act in the past, it would be far more difficult to act now as if nothing of any consequence had occurred.

The horses were harnessed to the phaeton once again, and by the time they set off it was growing late in the afternoon.

The country was very beautiful. There was no wind and it was therefore comparatively warm. There were primroses under the hedgerows and the daffodils were showing their golden trumpets among the young grass in the meadows.

Cassandra was telling herself that she almost hated the Duke, when he turned his head to look at her and say softly:

"When I look at you, I think you are spring and in some magical manner you can disperse for me the darkness of winter."

There was a note in his voice that made her heart seem to turn over in her breast. She longed to move closer to him, to rest her head against his shoulder.

'What does it matter what happens tomorrow?' she asked herself wildly, 'as long as we can have today?'

He was near her, and when he spoke to her with just that note in his voice and that particular expression in his eyes, the only thing that mattered was that they were together.

They travelled for miles down twisting lanes, along cart-tracks and through woods to the top of a hill where they could look over the valley towards the Chiltern Hills.

They spoke of many superficial things, but Cassandra knew that they were conscious only of each other's hearts.

Something magical had happened! Something which drew them closer to each other every second, until she felt, although he had not touched her, she was in his arms, and that with every word he spoke, he kissed her lips.

Then all too soon the sun was beginning to sink in the West, the sky was a kaleidoscope of colour and below them was a huge stone mansion, its roofs impressively ornate above the trees which surrounded it.

"Is that the house?" Cassandra asked.

"It is," the Duke replied briefly.

Cassandra thought as they drew nearer that it was typical of Lord Carwen to own a place which seemed to symbolise importance, pomposity and wealth.

The green lawns with their stereotyped flower beds; the gold-tipped iron gates; the yew hedges fashioned by topiary work into travesties of nature, seemed to her to reveal the character of their owner.

She was sure of this when they entered the huge Hall, where half a dozen footmen in a grandiose livery bedecked with gold braid, were in attendance.

"His Lordship lives in style," Cassandra commented as she and the Duke followed an imposing MajorDomo down wide corridors hung with valuable pictures.

They reached a large Drawing-room and Cassandra saw Lord Carwen detach himself from a small group of people centred round the mantel-piece at the far end of it.

He advanced towards them.

Taking Cassandra's hand in his he raised it to his lips.

"May I welcome you to my home, pretty lady?" he said with a look in his eyes which she particularly disliked.

She curtsied and withdrew her hand from his with some difficulty.

"Varro, my dear boy," Lord Carwen said to the Duke, "you know you are always welcome. I think you know everyone who has arrived so far, but I must introduce Sandra."

By the time Cassandra was able to go upstairs for a short rest before dinner more guests had arrived.

They were mostly men, with a few exceptions of Lord Carwen's age and on intimate terms with him.

He chaffed them in a manner which Cassandra felt was vaguely insulting to her and the other women present.

It was not the way she would have expected her father to speak in a lady's presence, and then she realized that to Lord Carwen she was not a lady!

She was not certain either how to place His Lordship's other female guests.

There was a very attractive woman of about thirty-five, obviously well-born, who was flirting with sophisticated expertise with the Earl of Wilmere.

He was a middle-aged man and responded with bursts of loud laughter. The innuendos in most of the things he said were lost on Cassandra.

They kept referring to episodes when 'we did this' and 'we did that', and seemed so intimate that Cassandra innocently thought they were man and wife.

When she accompanied the other ladies upstairs to find their bed-rooms, she said, making polite conversation:

"Do you and your husband live in the country?"

The woman, who Cassandra later found was called Lady McDonald, laughed derisively.

"He is not my husband!" she exclaimed. "I only wish he were, and poor old Jimmy wishes it too! But unfortunately he has a dragon of a wife and six extremely tiresome children!"

Cassandra's eyes widened in astonishment.

"How is your husband, Julie?" one of the other women asked.

"As boring as ever," Lady McDonald replied, "wrapped in tartan and his pride in the frozen North."

"He still refuses to divorce you?"

"He is adamant about it!" Lady McDonald answered. "Says there has never been a scandal in the family since Robert the Bruce liaised with the Spider!"

Her laughter at her own joke echoed round the Hall. Cassandra was shocked. Then she told herself that it was exactly what she might have expected.

After all, both Lord Carwen and the Duke thought that she was an actress, and an actress would certainly not have been invited to a house-party together with someone like her mother or indeed with any lady of her acquaintance.

'It will be amusing to see how these sort of people behave,' she told herself.

At the same time she knew that the manner in which the gentlemen had joked not only amongst themselves, but with Lady McDonald and the other women downstairs had made her feel embarrassed.

She learnt that more guests would be arriving much later in the evening after the theatres closed.

There would be Lily Langtry and Freddy Gebhard, besides, judging by what Lord

Carwen said, several well-known figures from the Gaiety and the leading lady of Daly's Theatre.

"We shall be quite a packed house," Lady McDonald said as they reached the top of the staircase. "Now, let us see where everyone is sleeping."

Lying on a table on the wide landing was a plan of the bed-rooms.

Cassandra looked at it and thought she had never before seen such a thing at any house at which she had been a guest.

There was always a plan of the Dining-table so that guests could go straight to their places without having to wander around the table looking for the card on which their name was inscribed.

But to have the bed-rooms planned in such a manner was something new!

She saw that the majority of rooms were arranged in suites; her own, which was named "The Blue Room", had a Boudoir and Dressing-room attached.

She saw it was not far away from "The Master-Suite", and that the Duke was only just round the corner in what was entitled "The Red Room".

Lady McDonald was commenting on the rooms which had been allotted to two people called Rosie and Jack.

"Jack will have to go out in the corridor," she giggled, "and if there is one thing he dislikes, it is having to do that!"

They all laughed, and Cassandra wondered why it should upset anyone to have to go into the corridor, especially one as well-heated and well-furnished as those that she saw on either side of the staircase.

But a great deal of the women's chatter was incomprehensible, and she was glad when she could retire to her own room and find that Lord Carwen's housemaids had unpacked for her.

She rang the bell and a maid came to undo her gown.

"Will you rest on the bed, Miss, or on the chaise-longue?" she enquired.

"On the bed," Cassandra answered.

She put on the silk wrap which Hannah had packed for her, and the maid having removed the bed-spread, she settled herself against the pillows and was covered by a satin eiderdown.

"I would like my bath an hour before dinner," she told the maid and shut her eyes.

She thought she might be able to sleep, because having been late last night she was in fact a little tired.

Instead she found herself thinking of the

Duke and the moment that he told her that he had fallen in love with her! She had known, even as he held her eyes spellbound, that he was speaking in all sincerity.

He was in love as she was in love!

They were drawn to each other and there was no escape.

'I want him to love me,' Cassandra admitted to herself. 'But I also want him to think that nothing else, not even money, is of importance beside our love.'

She thought of the bitterness in his face when he told her that his horses were to be sold at Tattersall's.

She wondered what else he had disposed of, and thought that Alchester Park must be filled with treasures that would fetch enormous sums of money in the London Salerooms.

'I want him to tell me the truth,' she thought. 'I want him to admit to me that he is marrying for money, and then perhaps I can tell him who I am.'

Yet again there came that little tremor of fear that he might be angry because she had deceived him.

She was still thinking of the Duke when the maid came back to light the gas-lamps, make up the fire, and bringing the bath in which Cassandra could bathe by the fire-side.

Lady Carwen might be in Paris, but she certainly provided every expensive luxury for her guests.

There were three different oils from which Cassandra could choose to scent the bath-water and the towels which were embroidered with a huge coronet smelt of lavender.

She noticed also that throughout the house there were bowls of pot-pourri obviously made, as her mother made hers at home, from the flowers in the garden.

The sheets and pillow-cases were edged with lace and there was an ermine rug lying on the chaise-longue.

The desk contained every possible facility for writing a letter.

There was a jewel-studded pen-holder, a blotter with gold corners, a writing-paper box in red leather. There was a clock with a face encircled by diamonds.

There was an onyx pen-tray, a tortoiseshell letter-opener, a calendar framed in polished silver, and innumerable other objects, all of which were designed to make letter-writing an Art.

There were also carnations and a profusion of yellow daffodils to decorate not only the bed-room but the adjacent Boudoir into which Cassandra peeped before she went downstairs.

"Which gown will you wear, Miss?" the maid enquired.

Quite suddenly Cassandra knew she could not go down flaunting one of the low-cut theatrical dresses she had bought from Chasemnore's.

She had a revulsion for the women who were already staying in the house.

There was no need for her to look at their exaggeratedly fashionable clothes to know that they were not the type of whom her mother would approve.

The way they laughed, the boldness of their eyes, their hands which seemed to be always reaching out to pat a masculine arm or to hold on to the lapel of a coat, were more revealing even than anything they said or wore.

Cassandra looked with distaste at the glittering green gown she had worn on the first night to Lord Carwen's party, at one of jonquil yellow and another of coral pink satin.

She pointed instead to one of her own gowns which Hannah had packed regardless of her protests.

It was exquisitely styled. The very soft lace which was draped over the front of the full skirt, swept backwards into quite a small bustle at the back, to fall in frills to the floor.

The *décolletage* was much higher and indeed correct for a young girl, but it revealed Cassandra's tiny waist and the perfect symmetry of her white arms.

Tonight she did not even attempt to open her jewel-case, and she asked the maid to arrange her hair in the exact manner in which Hannah had done it before she left London.

The long tresses of fire-touched gold were swept around her head to make it small and almost Grecian in shape.

But however subdued Cassandra might wish to appear, there was nothing she could do to conceal the brilliant blue of her eyes or the dark lashes which seemed too long to be natural.

Because she felt it might cause comment if she left her face untouched she flicked just a suspicion of powder onto her cheeks and put the faintest touch of salve on her lips.

"You look lovely, Miss, if I may say so!" the maid remarked.

"Thank you," Cassandra smiled.

"I have never seen a more lovely dress," the maid went on. "When I unpacked it, I thought it might be a wedding-gown!"

Cassandra turned towards the door.

"Thank you for helping me," she said and walked downstairs.

She felt a little nervous as a footman

opened the door of the Drawing-room.

It was a very attractive room lit by a great chandelier in the centre while candles in huge carved Italian candlesticks illuminated the rest of the room.

Lord Carwen had already said before dinner that he thought gas-light was ugly and that women looked their best by candlelight.

He was standing in front of the fireplace as Cassandra entered and she realised as she moved towards him that she was the first guest down to dinner.

"It seems I am a little early," she said quickly.

"You could never be too early for me."

As Lord Carwen spoke he took her hand and held it close against his lips.

Cassandra felt herself shiver from the warm possessiveness of his mouth, and she disliked even more the way his eyes looked at her. She thought she saw a touch of fire in them.

"You are very lovely," he said, "and I cannot tell you how happy it makes me to have you here in my own house. We have a lot to say to each other, little Sandra."

Cassandra was concerned with trying to take her hand from his grasp but he would not relinquish it.

"Please," she said insistently, a flush coming to her cheeks.

"Are you afraid that the others will come in and see us?" Lord Carwen asked. "In that case, Sandra, later we will go somewhere quiet where we can get to know each other."

He let her hand go as if reluctantly, and Cassandra walked quickly away from him towards the fireplace.

"I know," Lord Carwen said following her and standing too close, "that we are going to mean a great deal to each other, you and I."

"I think you are mistaken, My Lord," Cassandra answered firmly.

"I am never mistaken where a pretty woman is concerned," Lord Carwen said. "I knew as soon as I saw you, Sandra, you were someone I wished to know well — very well."

Cassandra turned her head away from him to look into the flames.

"I have a present for you which I know will please you," he said softly.

He looked at her bare neck and she felt as if he touched it with his fingers.

"You may tell me which is your favorite stone," he went on, "but I have already decided that diamonds become you best."

There was no mistaking the insinuation

behind his words and Cassandra moving away from him said formally:

"I never accept presents from — strangers, My Lord."

"We will not be strangers for long," Lord Carwen smiled.

She thought there was a confidence about him that was unassailable.

He was so sure of himself; so completely convinced that he could say or do as he wished and she would not rebuff him.

"I am afraid you are under a misapprehension," Cassandra said. "I am here because I am a friend of the Duke. You invited us together and it was a great pleasure to drive here with him in his phaeton. I hope that is clear?"

She wondered as she spoke if she had been too rude, considering that Lord Carwen was her host.

To her surprise he laughed!

"I like your spirit," he said, "but I assure you you will find me very much more generous than Alchester can afford to be, and the more I see you the more I am convinced that we shall get along very well together."

"You are mistaken, My Lord," Cassandra said sharply.

Then to her relief the Drawing-room door opened and the Duke came in.

She turned to him with what was almost a little cry of gladness and if she had not restrained herself, she would have run down the room to meet him.

She wanted to hold on to him to make sure he was there, to know that he would protect her, although she could hardly say that Lord Carwen's advances had been actually menacing.

And yet she was afraid!

She knew that, even as the Duke came to her side, for some inexplicable reason she was really very frightened.

Chapter Seven

Dinner was not so noisy or so gay as Cassandra had expected.

Since there were extra men, some of them had to sit together and they instantly began to talk sport. Even the Earl of Wilmere's normally unrestrained laughter seemed more subdued than it had earlier.

Cassandra was glad to find that she was not next to Lord Carwen.

Instead she was on the right of the Duke with a middle-aged man on her right. He was engrossed in talking about the shooting prospects for the coming year with the gentleman on his right.

Cassandra found herself thinking that the Duke was very quiet and she fancied that when he was not actually speaking to her there was a frown between his eyes.

She wondered if it had anything to do with the conversation that had taken place when he had come into the Drawing-room and found her alone with Lord Carwen.

She had been glad and relieved to see him, but she fancied that, as he advanced across the room, there was a grim expression on his face.

"I want to speak to you, Varro," Lord Carwen said as he reached the hearth-rug.

The Duke did not answer. He merely looked at his host expectantly.

"De Veet has arrived and I want you to be nice to him."

"I do not like him," the Duke replied in an uncompromising voice.

"That is immaterial!" Lord Carwen retorted.

"On the contrary, I think it is very pertinent to the matter in question," the Duke contradicted. "I am quite convinced that he is not to be trusted."

"That may be your opinion," Lord Carwen said, "but I have gone into the matter very thoroughly, and I can assure you, Varro, that your apprehensions are quite unfounded."

The Duke walked nearer to the fireplace and stood holding his hands out towards the fire as if he felt cold.

Then he said quietly:

"I am still not interested, Carwen."

Cassandra saw an expression of anger in Lord Carwen's eyes.

"Now look here, Varro —" he began, but before he could say any more the door opened to admit a number of other members of the house-party.

Several new guests appeared to have arrived while they were changing for dinner. Among them was Mr. De Veet, who Cassandra learned was a South African.

He was a heavy, coarse man, flashily dressed, who spoke with a decided accent. Looking at him perceptively, Cassandra was certain the Duke was right and he was not to be trusted.

She wondered why Lord Carwen was so anxious for the Duke to be nice to Mr. De Veet.

She came to the conclusion there must be some matter of business involved because Lord Carwen himself went out of his way to be almost over-effusive to his guest.

At dinner Mr. De Veet had two of the prettiest women in the party on either side of him.

Later, when Lord Carwen's theatrical guests arrived from London, it was obvious that the party was to be paired off, every man being more or less allotted a particular woman in whom he either already had, or was expected to take, an interest.

Dinner was so long drawn out with many courses, and the gentlemen lingered so long over their Port, that there was in fact little time to wait before Lily Langtry arrived with Freddy Gebhard.

They were followed shortly by the ladies of the theatre who, Cassandra learned, had been conveyed to the country by Lord Carwen's fastest horses.

Mrs. Langtry was looking very beautiful.

She arrived wearing full evening-dress with magnificent jewellery, and she looked so elegant without a hair out of place that she might have stepped from behind the footlights into the Drawing-room.

Everyone present paid her extravagant compliments and she greeted Cassandra with a charming smile, although it was obvious she was surprised to find she was staying in the house.

"I am grateful to you, Lily, for introducing me to the entrancing Sandra," Lord Carwen said. "But then your taste has always been impeccable."

"I understood it was Varro she wished to meet," Mrs. Langtry replied with what Cassandra felt was a hint of mischief in her eyes.

"Varro is also here," Lord Carwen remarked.

"How kind of you," Mrs. Langtry said with a little smile.

Cassandra thought there was a suggestion of sarcasm in her voice.

As soon as everyone had arrived, a room off the Drawing-room was opened to reveal a roulette table, in addition to which the guests could play Baccarat or Bridge.

It was obvious, Cassandra noticed, that the women were carrying no money with them and that the gentlemen were expected to act as their backers.

A great number of golden sovereigns were soon lying on the green-baize tables.

"Do you want to play?" the Duke asked.

Cassandra shook her head.

"I hate gambling!"

"Then let us sit by the fire," he suggested, and they remained behind in the Drawing-room while the rest of the party clustered round the tables in the Card-room.

"I think I shall go to bed soon," Cassandra said. "This is my third night of gaiety and I feel rather tired."

"You certainly do not show it," the Duke answered.

He looked at her sitting in a chair which framed the soft ivory lace of her gown. The golden lights in her red hair glittered in the candlelight and her eyes were very blue.

It seemed as if there was little they had to say to each other.

Yet Cassandra knew it was a joy beyond words to be with him; to feel that they were together, although they were surrounded by other people and in the house of a man she disliked.

She had a feeling the Duke was thinking the same thing.

Suddenly feeling shy of the expression in his eyes, she turned her head away to look into the fire.

"I was very happy today," the Duke said softly.

"It was . . . something I have never done . . . before," Cassandra said without thinking.

"What have you never done before?" the Duke enquired.

"Driven alone with a man and had luncheon at an Inn."

She was speaking more to herself than to him, and then she feared he might think it strange that as an actress she should not find such occasions quite ordinary.

He was about to say something when Lord Carwen came back into the Drawing-room.

"I wondered what had happened to you both," he said.

His tone was not accusing but perfectly pleasant.

"I do not gamble," Cassandra said quickly.

"Perhaps you do not know how to do so,"

Lord Carwen suggested. "Let me be your instructor."

"No, thank you," Cassandra replied. "Quite frankly I think it is a silly way of passing the time, when one might be talking or reading or doing something else more interesting."

"There I agree with you," Lord Carwen smiled.

He turned to the Duke.

"Varro, if you are really determined not to do as I have asked you with regard to De Veet, will you have a word with him? He had just told me that he is counting on you, so, if you have really changed your mind, I feel it would be a mistake to leave him in ignorance."

"I have not changed my mind," the Duke answered. "I told you from the beginning I do not wish to be associated with him."

"I am afraid I did not understand that," Lord Carwen said. "In fact I told De Veet that you would represent me on his Board."

"That is something I have no intention of doing," the Duke said sharply.

"Then, my dear fellow, you must make your attitude clear to De Veet. He is suffering under the same misapprehension as I was, that you were definitely interested in his proposition. I think you had better tell him now — at once — before things go any further."

"I should have thought tomorrow would be soon enough!"

Lord Carwen shook his head.

"If you are not prepared to play ball, dear boy, then I have every intention of asking Wilmere. He has been badgering me for some time to put him in touch with just such a chance to make money."

The Duke rose slowly to his feet.

"Very well, I will speak to De Veet. Are you coming with me, Sandra?"

"Yes, of course," she answered.

She rose and moved towards the Duke, then as he turned towards the door Lord Carwen said:

"One moment, Sandra, I have something to show you."

Both Cassandra and the Duke stopped still.

"What is it?" Cassandra asked.

"Nothing more sensational," Lord Carwen replied with a twist of his lips, "than a plan of my Estate. You were talking to Colonel Henderson about it at dinner, I believe."

"Yes, I was," Cassandra answered. "Did he tell you so?"

"He told me that you were interested in my Point-to-Point course that has been spoken of as a model of its kind. It certainly commanded a great deal of attention last week when we had our first meeting."

"Colonel Henderson described it to me," Cassandra said. "He told me your horses won two races."

"I should really thank Varro for that," Lord Carwen said agreeably. "He sold me the hunters and I was very pleased with their performance."

Cassandra glanced at the Duke and knew without his saying anything how much he must have disliked having to part with his precious hunters. Once again he must have been in pressing need of the money.

"I have the plans here on my desk," Lord Carwen said. "Let me show them to you."

There was nothing Cassandra could do but agree, and reluctantly the Duke walked away from her and into the Card-room.

Cassandra had no wish to be alone with Lord Carwen, but she felt she could not refuse to look at his plans without being extremely rude.

Moreover it was unlikely that he would try to be over-familiar while the rest of the party were in the next room and might interrupt them at any moment.

Lord Carwen drew from the drawer of a bureau inlaid with ivory a plan which was headed "The Lord Carwen Point-to-Point, March 15th, 1886".

"Now let me show you why this is different from the usual Point-to-Point Course —" Lord Carwen began conversationally.

He spread the plan out as he spoke, and Cassandra with her experience of her father's private Steeplechase course at The Towers realised that it was in fact very well planned.

"Unlike most Point-to-Points," Lord Carwen continued, "the Judges here can keep an eye on the Competitors the whole way round, and of course it is more interesting for the spectators."

"What you have really devised," Cassandra said, "is a race-course."

"I suppose that is true," Lord Carwen said, "but I am not particularly interested in racing as such. It is Varro who thinks only of the 'Sport of Kings'."

"His father's horses were famous," Cassandra said, almost as if she were defending the Duke.

"Would you like to own a race-horse of your own?" Lord Carwen asked.

"Not particularly," Cassandra answered.

She wondered what Lord Carwen would say if she told him that her father owned a large number of race-horses and had promised her that as soon as she was twenty-one that she could race under her own colours.

"I wonder what you would like to possess," Lord Carwen said.

Cassandra did not answer.

She was aware that he was looking at her with that expression in his eyes which she most disliked. So she merely bent her head over the plans on the desk.

She traced with the tip of her finger the course the riders would follow; noted the height of the jumps; and was certain that they would prove of little difficulty as far as her new horses, Firefly and Andora, were concerned.

Lord Carwen suddenly set down in front of her on the plan an open jewel-case.

In it lay a broad diamond bracelet glittering in the light from the Chandelier.

For an instant Cassandra was still. Then she said coolly:

"I have already told you, My Lord, that I do not accept presents from strangers."

"I am not a stranger," Lord Carwen answered, "and you know as well as I do that diamonds are something every sensible girl should collect, besides being vastly becoming to a skin as white as yours."

"Thank you," Cassandra replied, "but my answer is no."

She would have turned away, but Lord Carwen caught her by the wrist.

"When you are as sweet to me as I wish you to be," he said softly, "I will give you a necklace to match the bracelet."

"You seem to find it very difficult to understand plain English," Cassandra replied. "How can I make you realise, My Lord, that I will not accept a gift of any sort from you? No diamonds, however large, however expensive, will tempt me to alter my decision."

"I suppose you fancy yourself in love with Varro?" Lord Carwen said, and now there was something like a snarl in his voice.

"That has nothing to do with it!"

"I think it has," Lord Carwen insisted. "But let me inform you that Varro can give you nothing while I am a very generous man!"

Cassandra tried to release herself but his fingers were still clasped tightly around her wrist.

She was not really afraid. She could hear the voices of the other guests as they crowded round the tables in the gambling room.

She knew Lord Carwen would not risk her calling out or making a scene.

"Let me go!" she said firmly but quietly.

"I cannot credit you are serious in refusing my presents," Lord Carwen answered making no motion to release her.

"You do not appear to listen to what I say."

"You are entrancing! You attract me more than any woman I have seen for years. It is not only that enticing red hair of yours, but the curl of your lips, the way your eyes glint under those long dark lashes."

"I do not wish you to say such things to me," Cassandra said. "I am here as your guest and I must ask you to treat me with courtesy."

Lord Carwen laughed.

"I have no desire to be courteous to you, Sandra. I want to make love to you; to kiss you; to awaken a response in that perfect little body of yours!"

He paused before he added:

"I cannot believe that anyone with hair the colour of yours would not be passionate in response to the desire you arouse in me."

"Again you are mistaken," Cassandra said, holding her chin high. "How can I make it clearer to Your Lordship? You simply do not attract me."

"But you attract me!" Lord Carwen retorted. "And as far as I am concerned, that is all that matters!"

"I see I made a mistake in accepting your hospitality," Cassandra said. "It would clearly be best if I asked His Grace to take me away tomorrow morning."

"You fascinate me by the challenge in your voice," Lord Carwen said, apparently quite unabashed. "You bewitch me with every word you say and every movement you make! You are adorable and very exciting, little Sandra!"

Once again Cassandra tried to free herself from the tight hold he had on her wrist.

"Shall I tell you something?" he asked.

She did not reply and he went on:

"Women always change their minds and I will make you change yours. I want you, Sandra, and I intend to have you! And let me tell you I am a very determined fighter."

"Then I am afraid, My Lord, that on this occasion you have met your Waterloo!" Cassandra answered coolly.

She twisted her arm unexpectedly and was free. Without another word she turned her back on him and walked away across the room.

She knew he was watching her and heard him laugh very softly underneath his breath.

'Why should I be frightened of him?' she asked herself. 'At the same time, I shall leave tomorrow morning.'

She found the Duke talking to Mr. De Veet in a corner of the Card-room. They were both looking cross, Cassandra thought, and the Duke's eyes lit up when he saw her.

She went to his side, resisting an impulse to hold on to him as if she needed his protection.

"I think it is time I went to bed."

"I quite agree," the Duke answered. "You have had a long day."

He turned towards Mr. De Veet.

"You must excuse me, De Veet. There is really no point in discussing it any further."

"Let me try to persuade Your Grace," Mr. De Veet answered in a guttural voice.

"It will be a waste of time!" the Duke said quietly.

He took Cassandra's arm and led her towards the door into the Hall; but before they had reached it they encountered Mrs. Langtry.

"I have lost a lot of Freddy's money," she said to the Duke, "and so the sooner I retire, the better. I never was a good gambler!"

"I dislike gambling in private houses," the Duke answered.

"I quite agree with you," Freddy Gebhard said, "and we are both tired. It must be very late."

The first move having been made, it appeared that most of the other people in the party were ready to do the same, and Cassandra walked up the stairs with Mrs. Langtry and most of the other ladies at the party.

It was impossible for her to have a last word with the Duke or even to say goodnight to him with everyone listening.

She wanted to tell him how Lord Carwen had behaved, but there was no opportunity.

The same maid came to her room to undo her gown, and when she was alone she brushed her hair and finally was ready to get into bed.

It was then a thought struck her and she walked to the door to turn the key in the lock. But there was no key!

She stared in perplexity remembering distinctly that she had noticed the key before she went down to dinner because it had been gold.

Gold keys and gold locks to the door, she had thought, were ostentatiously opulent! She had never in fact seen them before in any house in which she had stayed.

Now the key had gone!

She looked around apprehensively and went into the Boudoir next door.

'Perhaps,' she thought hopefully, 'the key for that door will fit the one in the bedroom.'

But once again there was no key!

Cassandra tried to tell herself:

'I must have been mistaken in thinking I saw a key before dinner.'

Yet she knew she had definitely noticed it because it had been ornate and in rather an attractive design.

She looked around the bed-room. There were two upright chairs that appeared to be fairly substantial despite the fact that they were covered in pale blue damask, with their frames carved and gilded.

She placed the back of one of the chairs under the handle of the door which led to the corridor, the other against the door which led into the Boudoir.

She remembered her Nanny doing the same years ago because she had always been afraid of burglars. At the same time the chairs Nanny used had always been heavy and of solid wood.

Cassandra hoped that the gold frames of these chairs would be just as effective.

'Anyway,' she told herself, 'I am being unduly apprehensive. I cannot believe that anyone would try to come into my room.'

With a sense of relief she remembered the Duke was not far away in the 'Red Room' which she had seen on the plan she had examined with Lady Macdonald.

He was sleeping just around the corner from the suite she occupied and she could, if necessary, reach him quite easily.

She got into bed and realised when she put her head down on the pillow that she was in fact very tired.

It had been difficult to sleep the night before because she had lain awake thinking about poor Nancy. The night before that it had been her thoughts of the Duke which had kept her awake until it was dawn.

Now she felt the soft warm waves of slumber creeping over her and in a very short while she was unconscious.

She awoke suddenly with a start, aware that some sound had awakened her.

She heard it again — a distinct knock on the door!

She sat up in bed. The fire had burned low but there was still enough light to see across the room and to realise that the doorhandle was being turned and only the chair was preventing the door from opening.

The door however did open a crack and she heard a voice say:

"Sandra, let me in!"

It was hardly more than a whisper and yet there was no need for her to guess who it was who spoke.

She felt as if she was unable to move.

She could only sit staring at the crack in the door; seeing the chair shake as it withstood a violent assault upon it.

Then suddenly she was terrified!

She was sure that the chair might give way at any moment.

"Sandra, let me in! I wish to talk to you."

There was no mistaking a command in the words, even though the voice was still kept low! Cassandra knew she must get away! She must escape while she still could!

It seemed to her that the crack was getting wider.

She thought the legs of the chair might break or it might slither across the carpet and was no longer an effective obstacle.

She was hardly conscious of what she was doing, but driven by a fear that was like a sword piercing through her she sprang from the bed.

Running across the room, she pulled aside the chair that she had placed in front of the door into the Boudoir.

She slipped through it and then passing the unlocked door which led into the passage opened the outer door on the other side of the room.

She could see her way by the light of a fire burning low in the grate and beyond the Boudoir she found a Dressing-room.

It was in darkness but she sped across it, being just able to discern a door facing the one by which she had entered.

She realised that this opened not on to the main corridor but on to a side passage and desperately she pulled it open.

Opposite she saw by the faint light of a gas-bracket the 'Red Room'.

Without thinking, without knocking, she turned the handle and went in . . .

The Duke had found his Valet waiting for him when he went upstairs to bed.

The man had been in his service for a long time; in fact he had been with the Alchester family since he was a boy.

"Your Grace's early. I wasn't expecting you for some hours," he remarked as the Duke entered the bed-room.

"You need not have stayed up, Hawkins."

"I always wait up for Your Grace."

"You have had to put up with a lot of dis-comforts in the past year," the Duke re-marked, "but this need not be one of them."

"I know m' duties, Your Grace!"

"And you have carried them out magnifi-cently, despite the difficulties."

"I've not minded that, Your Grace," Hawkins said. " 'Tis only we've all of us hated to see the house being run on a skeleton staff and the young ones having to leave the Estate."

"I know," the Duke said with a deep sigh, "but there was nothing I could do about it at the time."

"And now, Your Grace?"

"Things may get better — I am not certain."

"That's just what I says to the others, Your Grace, when they grumbles," Hawkins said. " 'Things'll get better,' I tell 'em, 'you mark my words. Master Varro won't let us down'."

"I wish I could be sure of that," the Duke remarked in a strange tone.

He watched the Valet open a cupboard in the panel-lining and put his shoes inside. Then the man went to the large wardrobe and hung up his evening-jacket.

"Well, there's money to burn in this place," Hawkins remarked. "But it's not a happy house, Your Grace."

"Why not?" the Duke enquired.

"I've always said, Your Grace, for a house to be a home, it needs a lady to run it. From what I hears, Her Ladyship's never here, and His Lordship fills the place with all sorts and kinds. Not that I intend to be disrespectful, if you take my meaning."

"I take your meaning, Hawkins. You

always were one to call a spade a spade!"

"Yes, indeed, Your Grace. At what time do you wish to be called?"

"At about eight o'clock," the Duke replied.

"Very good, Your Grace," Hawkins said. "Good-night to you."

"Good-night, Hawkins."

The Duke, wearing a long robe of heavy silk frogged with braid, picked up the "*Times*" which was lying on a side-table and sat down in an arm-chair by the fire.

He opened the newspaper but he did not in fact read it. Instead he laid it on his lap and sat staring into the flames.

He was thinking of what Hawkins had said.

He knew the man was speaking the truth when he said that the employees at Alchester Park were relying on him to restore to them the comfort and security they had known all their lives.

No-one resented more than the servants that the house was in a dilapidated state, repairs were not done, damp was coming in, and the whole place looked shabby and unkempt.

There had been a reason for Hawkins saying Lord Carwen's house needed a mistress to look after it and his meaning had not escaped the Duke.

He sighed again, a deep sigh that seemed to come from the very depths of his being.

Then, almost as if he forced himself away from his own thoughts, he opened the "*Times*" again to read the leading article.

He was almost half-way through it when the door opened.

He glanced up casually thinking that Hawkins must have returned and saw Cassandra!

She stood for a moment looking at him. Then hastily she shut the door behind her and he saw that her hands were trembling.

She wore only her night-gown which was of very fine lawn trimmed with lace.

It was the type of night-gown she had worn all her life, buttoned demurely to the neck, with a small flat collar, and long sleeves which ended in lace-trimmed frills that fell over her hands.

Her hair was loose and fell in red-gold waves over her shoulders. She looked very young, little more than a child, and her face was white with fear.

The Duke rose to his feet.

"What is it? What has upset you?" he asked.

He realised she was finding it difficult to reply.

"L . . . Lord Carwen . . . he is t . . . trying . . . to get into . . . my b . . . bed-room!" she stammered breathlessly.

Then with a little cry she turned towards the door.

"He will r . . . realise I have c . . . come . . . here. I left the door of the . . . Dressing-room o . . . open."

For a moment they looked at each other. Then Cassandra whispered:

"Hide me . . . he must not . . . find me . . . !"

"No, of course not," the Duke said, and his voice was calm and matter-of-fact.

"Shall I g . . . get into . . . the w . . . wardrobe?"

Even as she spoke they heard footsteps, and swiftly the Duke opened the cupboard in the paneling into which Hawkins had put his shoes.

Without making a sound, Cassandra slipped past him and he closed the door behind her.

He hardly had time to take the few steps back to the hearth before the door of the room opened and Lord Carwen stood there.

He too was wearing a long robe over his night-shirt. The dark red of it seemed to echo the flush on his heavy face, and to accentuate the suspicion in his eyes.

"Hello, Carwen," the Duke exclaimed in a surprised tone. "Is anything wrong?"

Lord Carwen looked around the room.

Then as if he spoke deliberately choosing his words with care he replied:

"I came to see if you were quite comfortable, Varro. I hope you are being properly looked after?"

"I have my Valet with me."

"Yes, of course," Lord Carwen said. "But my staff are often extremely careless about details. I suppose there are hangers in your wardrobe?"

As he spoke he pulled open the door and glanced inside. Then he shut it again and moving across the room looked behind the heavy damask curtains which covered the window.

"I am always finding sash-cords broken and — blinds which do not work," he muttered.

"I have always thought that everything in your house was perfection," the Duke remarked.

Lord Carwen came and stood beside him in front of the fire.

"If there is any — suggestion of your leaving tomorrow," he said, "I hope you will remember that I particularly want you here for dinner."

"But of course," the Duke answered. "I

thought Sandra and I were staying until Monday."

"You are!" Lord Carwen said positively.

He looked at the Duke for a moment. Then he said:

"By the way, Varro, I rather fancy little Sandra, and quite frankly, my dear boy, you cannot afford her!"

The Duke did not answer and after a moment Lord Carwen went on:

"Soiled doves of her type prove very expensive, as I am sure you know. I am prepared to offer her a house of mine which has recently become vacant in St. John's Wood, and of course her own carriage."

"Have you suggested to Sandra that she should become your mistress?" the Duke asked and there was a steely note in his voice.

"She is at this moment showing a provocative reluctance," Lord Carwen admitted, "which, needless to say, has exactly the effect she intends! It increases my ardor and my determination to possess her in the end!"

He laughed and it was not a pleasant sound.

"Women are all the same, Varro. They all believe that to play 'hard-to-get' increases their price, and in the majority of cases it does!"

"You sound very sure of yourself," the Duke said. He spoke slowly with an intentional lack of expression.

"I am sorry to cut you out, dear boy," Lord Carwen smiled, "but I can assure you that your interest in this little butterfly was bound to be short-lived."

He paused to say impressively:

"Diamonds are expensive, but very rewarding, as our friend Lily knows! Sandra is well aware on which side her bread is buttered and I feel quite certain you will not put any obstacles in my way."

"Are you so certain of that?" the Duke asked.

"Quite certain!" Lord Carwen replied positively. "I could make things very difficult for you, Varro. Like the villain in a melodrama, I can always foreclose on the mortgage, or refuse to extend your loan!"

He laughed again.

"But I do not think there need be any dramatics between us. Just fade out of the picture where Sandra is concerned! I shall take your place very ably and with an expertise which at your age you undoubtedly lack."

"Perhaps the lady in question might have something to say about it," the Duke suggested.

"She may prevaricate a little," Lord

Carwen replied. "She was astute enough this evening to refuse a diamond bracelet I offered her — doubtless holding out for the necklace, the ear-rings and the brooch to go with it!"

He paused to add:

"However, I consider it to be worth my while to pursue the matter. So as far as you are concerned, Varro, it is good-bye."

"You have made yourself very clear," the Duke said.

There was an ice in his voice that Lord Carwen did not pretend to misunderstand.

"Look elsewhere," he said, putting his hand on the Duke's shoulder, "and you will find me as accommodating in the future as I have been in the past. I am a good friend, Varro, but a bad enemy! Good-night!"

He walked across the room as he spoke, opened the door and closed it behind him.

The Duke waited. Then, as he saw the door in the paneling open, he held his fingers to his lips.

He stood quite still until some seconds later he heard footsteps going down the passage.

Only then did he cross to the door and turn the key in the lock.

He turned round to see Cassandra, having come from her hiding-place, standing white-faced and trembling, her eyes on his.

Then she moved towards him and hid her face against his shoulder.

"Take me . . . away! Take me away now . . . at once!" she pleaded.

The fear in her voice was very obvious and the Duke could feel her body trembling beneath the fine lawn of her night gown.

He put his arms round her and heard her whisper, her voice muffled against his shoulder:

"I did not . . . know . . . I did not . . . understand . . . that anyone could be . . . like that . . . could say such things!"

The Duke reached out towards the bed and pulled off the silk coverlet.

Wrapping it around Cassandra's shoulders like a shawl, he moved her towards the fire and sat her down, almost as if she were a child or a doll, in the wing-backed armchair.

She looked at him wide-eyed, her face very pale, and her hands which had clasped the bed-spread around her were shaking.

"Take me . . . away!"

"I will do that," the Duke answered speaking for the first time. "But there are some questions I want to ask you."

"Q . . . questions?"

Her eyes were dark with fear.

"Yes, and I want the truth, Sandra."

She did not answer, surprised by the sternness of his face and the manner in which his eyes looked into hers. He seemed to be seeking, searching into the very depths of her heart.

"What is . . . it?" she asked, more frightened than she had been before.

"Who was with you in your flat last night?"

"My . . . maid."

"Is that the truth?"

"Yes . . . Hannah was with me . . . she is always with me . . . when I am in the . . . flat."

"Have you ever had a lover?" the Duke's words seemed to vibrate through the air.

For a moment Cassandra did not comprehend what he meant. Then the colour flooded over her pale face, rising from her chin up to her forehead to recede again, leaving her paler than she had been before.

"N . . . no . . . of course not . . . how c . . . could you think such a . . . how c . . . could you i . . . imagine . . . ?"

The words came brokenly between her lips. It seemed to her that he thought of her as if she were Nancy.

There was an expression on the Duke's face which she did not understand. Then he said, although now his tone was not so fierce:

"Where did you get your jewellery? Who gave it to you?"

"My father . . . except for the pearls . . . they belong to my . . . mother."

The Duke looked at her for a long moment and then he said quietly:

"I believe you! Oh, my darling, you do not realise what I have been imagining, how much it has tortured me!"

He saw that she was so bemused by what had occurred that she did not really take in what he was saying.

Then in a tone of voice which was now kind and comforting, he said:

"I will take you away, but not tonight. We will leave first thing tomorrow morning. Have you brought a riding-habit with you?"

"Y . . . yes."

"Then we will rise early, borrow two horses from His Lordship without asking his permission, and ride across country. There is something I wish to show you."

"Could we go . . . now?"

The Duke shook his head.

"It is too late and might cause comment amongst the servants. But I promise you we will leave before anyone else in the house-party is awake."

He saw a light come into Cassandra's eyes. Then like a child who was still frightened of the dark, she said frantically:

"I cannot . . . go back to my . . . room . . . I cannot sleep . . . there."

"No, of course not," the Duke answered. "Wait here a moment."

He walked to the side of the bed, lit a candle and carrying it in his hand opened another door.

He was gone only a moment or two. When he returned he said:

"Come with me!"

She rose to her feet, still clutching the bed-spread around her. The silk of it rustled as she walked towards him.

Without touching her he led the way across the Sitting-room which she had suspected was next to his and through another door which led into a Dressing-room.

There was a large comfortable bed, but it was not so impressive as the one in the room which the Duke was using.

The Duke set the candle down on a bed-side table, then walked across the room to turn the key in the door which opened on to the corridor.

"Now listen, Sandra," he said. "When I have gone, lock the door behind me. Do you understand? You will be quite safe here and no-one can possibly disturb you until the morning."

Cassandra glanced around as if to convince herself that he was speaking the truth. Then she said nervously:

"Will you . . . leave the door of your . . . room open, just in . . . case I am . . . frightened?"

"It will be open," the Duke promised with a faint smile.

He looked at her.

In the candle-light she was very young and very vulnerable.

"You will be quite safe," he said reassuringly. "Tomorrow morning I will knock on the door at about half-past six. When you are dressed, we will go down to the stables, get our horses and be away long before anyone else has been called."

"Can we . . . really do . . . that?"

"We will do it!" he promised. "But we have a long ride ahead of us, so try to sleep. For I do not want you to collapse on the way!"

"I will not do that," Cassandra answered.

"Then good-night," the Duke said, "and lock the door behind me."

For a moment they looked into each other's eyes. Then abruptly he turned away and without saying another word left the room.

In the Sitting-room he stood listening

until he heard the sound of the key turning in the lock.

With a sigh he walked on into his own bed-room.

Chapter Eight

"We have escaped!" Cassandra told herself triumphantly as she and the Duke rode their horses away from the stables, and, keeping out of sight of the house, moved into the Park.

The morning was sunny and fresh and the horses were frisky, so for the time being there was no chance for conversation.

But Cassandra was exultant to know that she was again alone with the Duke and free from the menace of Lord Carwen.

She had thought it would be impossible to sleep last night. But she had been already very tired when she went to bed, and the shock of what occurred later naturally had taken its toll of her strength.

Instead therefore of lying awake as she had expected, fearful and apprehensive, she had slept dreamlessly until she was awakened by a knock at the door.

For one second her fears came flooding back over her, and then she realised that day-light was coming through the sides of the curtains.

"Are you awake, Sandra?" she heard the Duke ask softly.

She got out of bed and picked up the silk counterpane in which he had wrapped her the night before. She put it once again around her shoulders and going to the door unlocked it.

He was standing in the Sitting-room fully dressed and wearing riding-breeches.

"It is half past six."

She smiled at him and he wondered how many other women of his acquaintance would have been quite unself-conscious about their looks at that hour of the morning.

Cassandra's red hair was tumbled; her eyes were still sleepy; and there was a faint flush on her cheeks.

"I have looked into your bed-room," the Duke said quietly, "and you can feel quite safe. Will it take you long to get dressed?"

"I will be as quick as I can," she answered breathlessly.

The Duke opened the door of the Sitting-room and she saw that it led into the same passage that she had crossed the night before from her Dressing-room to his bed-room.

The gas-lights were extinguished and the empty passage was dim, but it was still easy to see the way to the open door of the Dressing-room.

Cassandra, with a sense of urgency, ran to

the bedroom she had left so fearfully the night before.

The door into the corridor was closed but she could see that it had been opened.

The chair had been moved and was standing a little away from the door, its gilded frame damaged from the manner in which it had been thrust aside.

Because she was so anxious to get away quickly, Cassandra did not try to think now of what had happened.

She washed quickly in cold water, found her riding-habit in the wardrobe and put it on.

It was a little difficult to fasten it herself because Hannah had packed her very latest and smartest habit from Busvine.

It was the habit-bodice which was widely advertised as being extremely becoming to the female figure and made so that no fastenings were visible.

It was in fact a riding-dress rather than a skirt and jacket, and was what all the fashionable lady riders had taken to wearing in the warmer months of the year.

The plain black of the material, with just a touch of white at the throat and wrists, was severe and yet extremely becoming to Cassandra.

As she dressed herself hastily, she had no

time to notice the translucent whiteness of her skin or how her red hair, braided neatly around her head to wear under the black topper, glowed in the morning sunshine.

Instead she tucked a handkerchief into the pocket of her skirt, and only as she turned to run back to the Duke the way she had come did she wonder what she should do about her clothes and jewellery.

As if he anticipated that this was the question she would ask, or perhaps their minds were so attuned to each other that he knew what she was thinking, he answered the question as soon as she reappeared in the Sitting-room.

"You have been very quick," he said approvingly. "Do not worry about your other things. I have left a note with my Valet to have them all packed and taken to London with mine."

"Then can we go?" Cassandra asked.

"At once," he replied with a smile.

Despite the fact that she supposed everyone must still be sleeping so early in the morning, Cassandra tiptoed along the corridor behind the Duke.

He ignored the wide staircase which led down into the Hall and instead led the way down several corridors until they came to another narrower staircase.

Descending it, the Duke continued through less formal parts of the house until finally they emerged into the open through a door off the kitchen, finding that it was only a few minutes away from the stables.

The Duke ordered the horses he required with an authority which Cassandra thought would have infuriated Lord Carwen if he had known what was happening.

Two magnificent horses, one a black stallion, the other a roan, were saddled and brought by the grooms into the yard.

The Duke said nothing, but Cassandra seeing the expression on his face exclaimed:

"They were yours!"

"Yes," he answered briefly, "they were mine."

The grooms were listening and Cassandra could say no more.

She wondered why the Duke had sold his animals to Lord Carwen rather than put them up at Tattersall's.

She could not help feeling that if her father had seen either of these horses and known to whom they belonged, he would have been willing to pay a very large price for them.

But what was important at the moment was that they should be clean away from the house and its owner.

Once they were out of the Park, the Duke led the way over the fields into the open countryside. Since their horses were fresh, they both realised without words that the first thing was to give them their heads.

They must have galloped for nearly two miles before the horses automatically slowed their pace and Cassandra looked at the Duke with laughter in her eyes.

"That has swept away the morning mists!"

"And your fears?"

"For the moment."

He looked at her shining eyes and flushed cheeks, as he said:

"You ride better than any woman I have ever seen. I was half-afraid that Juno would be too strong for you to hold, but I see I need have had no anxiety on that score."

"Where are we going?" Cassandra asked.

"To my home," the Duke answered. "I want you to see it."

"I would love that!"

As she spoke with a little lilt in her voice, she remembered the long article about Alchester Park that she had cut out from an illustrated magazine and stuck into the Album.

Now at last she would see the house of which she had read so much, and which was the birth-place and the background of the man she loved.

When they had ridden for another hour the Duke said:

"Do you see that Inn ahead of us? I think we would both enjoy breakfast. I know I am hungry!"

"So am I," Cassandra agreed.

The Inn with a thatched roof stood on the edge of a village green.

The Landlord was not unnaturally surprised to receive such obviously important guests so early in the morning, but ushered Cassandra and the Duke into a small private parlor where a maid-servant quickly kindled the fire.

There was a mirror on one wall of the room, and going towards it Cassandra took off her hat and tidied away the small tendrils of red-gold curls that had escaped from the tidy plaits.

Then she sat down at the round table opposite the Duke and the Landlord came hurrying in with eggs and bacon, home-cured ham, and a huge pork-pie besides newly-baked bread, honey in the comb and a huge pat of golden butter.

"Oi'm afraid we've only simple fare to offer ye, Sir," he said to the Duke.

"It looks very palatable," the Duke replied agreeably.

He refused ale or cider and instead drank the fragrant coffee that had been brewed for Cassandra.

"Food always tastes good when one has taken exercise," Cassandra said. "I have not eaten such a big breakfast since I was last out hunting."

She realised as she spoke that it was hardly in character for an actress to hunt. But the words were spoken and she could not unsay them.

To cover the slip she had made she went on hastily:

"I think perhaps I am hungry mostly because I am so relieved to get away from that horrible house and those even more horrible people. I thought when we arrived last night that it would be interesting to study them and see what they were like. I know now that I never want to see any of them again."

"Why were they such a surprise?" the Duke asked.

"I suppose I did not realise . . . before that women who are born . . . ladies, like Mrs. Langtry and Lady McDonald, would go everywhere with a man who was . . . not their . . . husband."

The Duke did not say anything but his eyes were on her face.

After a moment Cassandra said almost as

272

if she was talking to herself:

"My father told me that gentlemen liked to take pretty actresses out to supper and give them presents. I thought it was just because she was . . . beautiful that Mrs. Langtry had so many . . . diamonds, but . . . perhaps that is not the only . . . reason."

"Why did you think Lord Carwen was offering you the diamond bracelet?" the Duke asked quietly.

Cassandra tried to meet his eyes and failed.

Looking down at the table she said:

"I heard you asking him . . . last night if he had . . . suggested to . . . me that I become his . . . mistress."

Her voice trembled before she went on:

"I did not . . . understand that was . . . what he meant."

"What does your father do?" the Duke enquired.

Once again it seemed to Cassandra that he was changing the subject for some reason of his own.

She wondered wildly what her reply should be. It was obvious the Duke did not suppose her father was a gentleman of leisure as were the majority of his acquaintances.

"Father has some . . . land," she answered at length.

It was not a very adequate way of describing the 20,000 acres that Sir James Sherburn owned.

"So he farms?" the Duke said.

Cassandra nodded. That at least was true.

"Then you did not go on the stage because you needed the money. Was it because you found the country dull and you wanted excitement?"

Cassandra did not answer.

She had suddenly felt ashamed of the part she had acted to deceive the Duke. She wanted to tell him the truth and yet she could not bring herself to do so.

He had said yesterday that he was in love with her but he had not said it again.

Last night when she had been so frightened, he had treated her as he was treating her now, as if he were her brother rather than a man in love.

She rose from the table and walked across the room to the mirror, picking up her hat as she did so from the chair on which she had left it.

"I think we should be going," she said. "You said we had a long ride. I suppose we are returning to London tonight?"

"Were you expecting to do anything else?" the Duke asked.

"No, of course not," Cassandra said quickly.

The Duke paid for their breakfast and they mounted their horses in the yard and set off again.

There was no more beautiful time of year, Cassandra thought, than in Spring. The buds on the trees were vividly green, and were echoed in the colour of the young grass in the meadow-land.

They rode through woods where there were violets shyly showing their purple and white heads from under the dark-green leaves, and primroses on the mossy banks were sun-shine yellow.

There were anemones so fragile they seemed like fairy flowers against the trunks of the dark pine or the white of the silver birch.

They rode beside streams winding their way beneath weeping willows. Sometimes there were purple hills in the distance, and at others flat lush valleys where fat cows grazed contentedly.

Just as Cassandra was beginning to think it was time for another meal, they rode between two high iron gates with heraldic stone lions rampant on either side of them. Ahead lay a long drive lined with ancient oak trees.

It was obvious that the drive was un-tended, half covered with moss, and no-one had swept away the broken branches which had fallen in the winter gales, or cut the grass beneath the trees.

The trees ended and ahead of them she saw Alchester Park!

It had appeared large and awe-inspiring in its pictures, but in reality it had a warmth that could not be translated into pen and ink.

The brown red bricks within which it had been built in the reign of Queen Elizabeth had mellowed with age and glowed rosy in the sun.

There were towers and chimney-pots silhouetted against the sky, glittering diamond-paned windows and a wide flight of ancient stone steps led up to the great oak door with its huge ornamental hinges and studded with iron nails.

"It is lovely!" Cassandra exclaimed. "Far lovelier than I expected."

The lawns surrounding the house were not as smooth as they should have been and were badly in need of cutting, but Cassandra realised that if they were trimmed they would look like velvet.

The almond trees were in bloom as were the yellow jasmine flowers climbing over the red brick walls of what she suspected might be an herb-garden.

The Duke had drawn his horse to a standstill, but he made no effort to dismount.

He sat for a moment looking at the house and then he said:

"I think we had best take our horses to the stables. It is doubtful if anyone will have heard us arrive. Most of the few servants I have left are deaf anyway."

He turned the stallion's head as he spoke and trotted ahead of Cassandra until they came to the stables situated on the West side of the house.

Here there were long rows of stalls which Cassandra could see were empty.

When the Duke shouted an old groom emerged from one of them. His eyes lit up when he saw the Duke and he touched his forelock respectfully.

" 'Morning, Ye Grace. I did not know ye were a-coming home today."

"Neither did I," the Duke replied, "and I am not staying. See to these horses, Ned. We shall be needing them later this afternoon."

"Why, 'tis Juno and Pegasus!" the old man exclaimed delightedly, " 'tis fine to see 'em again, Ye Grace."

"I am afraid they will not be staying with us," the Duke said, and his voice was hard.

He helped Cassandra down from the

saddle and for a moment she was in his arms, but she knew he was thinking not of her but of his horses.

Because she could not bear to see the pain in his eyes, she walked ahead of him towards the house.

They went in through a side door which was open and the Duke led her down a passage which led into the main Hall.

The panelling was the beautiful silver-grey of oak that has matured over the years. The sun coming through the heraldic coats-of-arms on the glass windows cast strange shadows on the floor.

It gave the place a mystic appearance and the whole house seemed to Cassandra to have an atmosphere that was sweet, calm and happy.

She looked at the exquisitely carved oak staircase curving up to the floor above.

The heraldic newels on the staircase had once been painted in brilliant colours. Now they were scratched and faded, but they still had an inescapable charm that nothing new could have equalled.

"I expect you would like to wash," the Duke said. "You will find a bed-room at the top of the staircase. I will go and order something for luncheon."

Cassandra walked up the staircase. It was

so beautiful that she felt she should be wearing a gown of satin with an Elizabethan ruff high against her red hair, and long strings of huge pearls.

The bed-room too was lovely.

Beneath a painted ceiling a carved four-poster bed was hung with embroidered curtains. The walls were papered in a Chinese design and the pelmets above the curtains had strange golden birds rioting amongst exotic flowers.

It was, however, impossible not to notice that the carpet was threadbare and the curtains were torn and faded at the sides until there was no colour left.

There seemed also to be a sparsity of furniture which Cassandra guessed had once stood against the walls.

She took off her hat and washed her face and hands in the china basin which stood on an elegant washstand carved in peach-wood.

As she did so she suddenly realised that in her hurry to be away from the house she had put no colour on her lips, nor had she used any powder.

'I doubt if he will notice,' she told herself.

At the same time when she looked in the mirror she realised that she now looked younger than when she had been using cosmetics.

She was still looking at herself when she heard a knock at the door.

"Come in," she said, thinking that it might be a house-maid.

But it was the Duke.

"I thought you might like to take off your riding-boots," he said, "so I have brought you a jack."

Cassandra saw that he held in his hand a wooden jack which every horseman used to facilitate the removal of high boots.

"Oh, thank you!" Cassandra exclaimed.

The Duke set the jack down on the floor, and then as Cassandra walked towards it she exclaimed:

"But I have no slippers with me!"

"I did not think of that!" the Duke said, "but I am sure I can find you a pair."

He disappeared. Cassandra pulled off her long boots and knew she would be more comfortable without them.

At the same time she thought she would feel embarrassed at walking about without any slippers on her feet.

She had been waiting for several minutes when the Duke returned.

He walked in through the open door holding in his hands a pair of heel-less black slippers with a little rosette on the front of them, very similar to a pair Cassandra owned herself.

"I am sure these will fit you," he said confidently.

Then as she looked at them Cassandra suddenly wondered to whom they had belonged.

He was a bachelor and the behavior of the women in the house-party last night came flooding into her mind.

She felt suddenly that she could not . . . she would not wear the shoes of some other woman, perhaps an actress whom the Duke had brought to his home.

"I do not want them!" she said turning her head away.

The Duke looked at her averted face in surprise.

"Why not?" he asked.

"I do not . . . wish to wear . . . them."

He dropped the shoes into the seat of a chair as he advanced towards Cassandra. He took her by the shoulders and turned her round to face him.

"Why do you speak like that?" he asked. "What are you thinking?"

Then suddenly he gave a little laugh.

"You are jealous! Oh, my foolish, ridiculous darling, you are jealous! But I promise you there is no need for you to be."

He pulled her close against him until as he tipped back her head, his mouth was on hers.

Just for a moment Cassandra was still with surprise.

Then as her lips were soft beneath the hardness of his, she felt something strange and wonderful flicker into life and rise into her throat so that it was almost impossible to breathe.

It was an ecstasy, a wonder like nothing she had ever imagined, she felt as if the sun flooded into the room and enveloped them in a blinding light.

She could think of nothing except that the Duke was kissing her and that was what she had always known it would be like.

It was a moment so ecstatic, so glorious, so utterly and completely wonderful that when at last he raised his head and looked down into her face, she was unable to move.

"I love you!" he said in his deep voice. "Oh, my sweet, how much I love you!"

She felt that she vibrated at the sound of his voice and then with a little inarticulate murmur, she turned her face and hid it against his shoulder.

"I feel as if I have loved you through all eternity," he said, "as if you have always been there in my life. Look at me, Sandra."

She was unable to obey and very gently he put his fingers under her chin and turned her face up to his.

"Why are you shy?"

"I always . . . thought that if you . . . kissed me it would be . . . wonderful," she whispered, "but not so . . . unbelievably . . . glorious!"

He looked at her searchingly and yet the expression in his eyes was very gentle.

"I would believe, if it were not incredible that this is the first time you have been kissed!"

"The . . . only . . . time!" Cassandra whispered.

"But why?" he asked.

As if the question was superfluous his lips found hers again.

He kissed her demandingly, insistently, and with a passion that made her feel as if he drew her very heart from her body and made it his.

Then as she felt herself quiver with the thrills which ran through her like quicksilver, the Duke released her.

He took his arms from around her so quickly that she had to hold on to him to steady herself.

She had no idea how beautiful she looked; her eyes wide and excited; her lips soft and trembling a little from his kisses; a faint flush on her cheeks; her neck very white against the severity of her riding-habit.

The Duke looked at her for a long moment and then he said almost harshly:

"For God's sake do not look at me like that! I have a lot of explaining to do, but first let us have something to eat, and then I want to show you the house."

His tone was so different from when he had spoken of his love, that Cassandra felt as if she had suddenly been shaken into wakefulness.

The Duke picked up the slippers from where he had dropped them into a chair.

"You can put these on," he said. "They belonged to my mother!"

"I am . . . sorry," Cassandra murmured.

He knew she referred to the fact that she had been suspicious of a previous owner.

"You could hardly think anything else," he said almost savagely, "seeing the type of company with which you had to associate last night."

Cassandra put the slippers on and followed the Duke down the staircase and into the Hall.

She felt as if he had suddenly erected a barrier between them, and yet in a way she knew it was inevitable and that sooner or later they both had to face the future.

A very old Butler served their luncheon in a long Elizabethan Dining-Hall with a minstrels' gallery and an oriel at one end of it.

They ate at a refectory table that was as old as the house itself and sat on high-backed carved oak chairs which had come into the family in the reign of Charles II.

The old servant apologised that there was not much to eat.

But a golden-brown omelet filled with fresh tomatoes was followed by pigeons stuffed with mushrooms. There was no pudding, but a big round cheese was served, which the Duke told Cassandra was a local specialty.

They talked of quite ordinary things while the old Butler shuffled around the table waiting on them, but they neither of them seemed very hungry, and Cassandra knew she was avoiding the Duke's eyes.

It was impossible, when she thought about it, not to thrill with the memory of how he had kissed her.

At the same time she had heard the harshness in his voice when he pushed her away from him, and she knew she was waiting in an agony of apprehension for what he would say to her when they were alone again.

She was afraid as she had never been

afraid before that he would tell her that they must say good-bye to each other; that their love could mean nothing because he must marry a woman for her money.

'How can I bear it?' Cassandra whispered to herself.

When finally they rose from the table and left the Dining-Hall, she felt as if every nerve in her body was tense in anticipation of what lay ahead.

But first the Duke took her round the house.

He showed her small, panelled Salons, the Great Chamber where once the Manorial Courts were held, the Armoury filled with flags and ancient weapons that had been collected over the years.

There were flags captured at the battle of Worcester; others by an Alchester who had fought with Marlborough in his campaigns; won by an Alchester who had fought with Wolfe in Canada and two more by another Duke who had served at Waterloo.

But there was a sparsity of furniture, no tapestries, and in the Drawing-room few objets d'art. When they reached the long Picture Gallery, it was to find the walls were bare.

The Duke said very little.

He only led Cassandra through room

after room until finally they came to the Library, and only there were the walls fully covered.

"The valuable editions have been sold," the Duke said sharply. "What is left is not worth the expense of carting them away."

She knew he was suffering and as she turned towards the fire which she saw had been newly-lighted, she said softly:

"Will you explain to me what has . . . happened?"

"Sit down," the Duke said abruptly, "because that is exactly what I am going to do."

Obediently Cassandra sat down in a chair by the fireplace. The Duke stood in front of the fire not looking at her but staring across the room.

"I do not know quite where to begin," he said, "but I want to make you understand that I was brought up to believe that this house and the Estate in which it stands was a great heritage."

"Indeed it is," Cassandra said.

"It was drummed into me almost from the moment of my birth," the Duke went on. "I was told it was my destiny and my duty to expend my whole energy, my whole enthusiasm, my whole life, on being the 9th Duke."

Cassandra looked at him remembering

their conversation of the other night.

"So inevitably you . . . hated the idea."

"Not exactly," the Duke answered, "but it made me long for freedom, to be myself, to be allowed to have an independent thought, apart from what was almost a straight-jacket into which I had to live my life."

Cassandra gave a little sigh. She was beginning to understand so many things the Duke had said to her.

"At first it did not seem quite so constricting as it did later," the Duke said. "I had the idea of going into the Foreign Office, believing I could have there a career of my own. Then I learnt that it was impossible: I had too many responsibilities here. Moreover it infuriated my father to think I should have any interests outside the sacred circle of the Alchester domain."

"So there was no escape?"

"None," the Duke answered in a hard voice. "I was also told that in the pattern of Royalty I had to marry money, so that the Estate could be kept up and I myself could live as befitted my rank."

"And you agreed?" Cassandra asked.

"My assent was taken for granted," the Duke replied. "My marriage was arranged by my father and I accepted it as something inevitable that must happen to me at some time in the future. Then I went around the world."

"That was important to you?"

"I realised that in other countries men of my age were making money by using their brains and their energy. In England it is considered degrading for a gentleman to work for a living. But that does not apply elsewhere."

His voice deepened.

"In Australia I saw a chance of making a fortune, and I found even greater opportunities when I reached South Africa."

He paused for a moment and Cassandra saw he was looking back into the past, recalling perhaps his enthusiasm at what he had discovered.

"I came back to England with ideas that I was certain could be the foundation stone for restoring the family fortunes."

"What . . . happened?"

"My father laughed at me, refused to invest one penny either in the mining possibilities I had envisaged in Australia or in the prospecting for gold that I was sure would prove to be a success in South Africa."

He was silent and Cassandra saw the bitterness in his face.

"So you could not do what you wanted to do."

"But I did!" the Duke answered. "I borrowed the money!"

Cassandra looked up at him.

"From . . . whom?" she asked her voice hardly above a whisper.

"Need you ask?" the Duke replied. "From Carwen. He offered me anything I wanted. He is a very rich man."

"And you trusted him?"

"He made himself very pleasant," the Duke said. "He listened to my ideas, he flattered and encouraged me. That was something I needed desperately at that particular moment."

"What happened?"

"I was making up my mind to tell my father the truth and to ask him to reconsider his decision and be my sponsor, when he died," the Duke said. "It was then I realised I was my own master — until I learnt how utterly impoverished the Alchester coffers were!"

Cassandra saw that it had been a shock, but she did not speak and after a moment the Duke went on:

"There were death duties, and my father had spent far more than he could afford on his horses — banking, I suppose, on being able to pay off all his debts through the rich marriage he had arranged for me."

There was so much sarcasm in his voice

that Cassandra drew in her breath.

"I realised that if I was to stand on my own feet I had to have money. I mortgaged part of the estate to Carwen. I sold everything that I did not consider a family heirloom. Then when the money was invested Carwen began to show himself in his true colours."

"What did he do?"

"He began to manipulate me as I had been manipulated all my life by my father. He used my name to further his own interests and insisted that I should be his representative on Boards which I considered to be shady. He also asked for security against the loans he had made me in my father's life-time."

"What did you give him?" Cassandra asked.

"Horses, among them those we rode today, a large amount of furniture and the family pictures," the Duke replied. "He deliberately took them off the walls so that every time I looked at the spaces where they had been I should feel under a deeper obligation to him!"

"He is despicable!" Cassandra cried.

"He is a sharp-headed business-man," the Duke replied, "and I was a fool to get into his clutches."

He was silent for a moment before he went on:

"I know that in a few years the money I have invested in Australia and South Africa will increase a thousand-fold. Already the reports from both countries are fantastic, but I cannot wait."

"Why not?" Cassandra asked.

"Because I cannot maintain the estate and pay the wages. Because I refuse any longer to be beholden to Carwen!"

He paused to say slowly:

"Now there is only one thing I can do."

"And what is that?" Cassandra asked and her voice seemed almost to have died in her throat.

"I can sell the house," the Duke answered, "pay off the mortgage and the monies that Carwen has loaned to me. That will leave enough to pension off the old retainers and provide cottages for their old age. What part of the estate is left will, in time, pay its way."

"Is there not . . . another alternative?" Cassandra asked hesitatingly.

"Of course there is," the Duke answered. "I can marry the heiress that my father procured for me. She wants my title — I want her money. A very sensible arrangement, you might say."

Cassandra did not speak and after a moment the Duke went on:

"I was prepared to do it. I had made up my mind that it would be better to be beholden to a woman — any woman — than to Carwen. And then you know what happened."

"What . . . happened?"

"I met you!"

For the first time he turned to look at her.

"Oh, God! Why did this have to happen to me now at this moment? And yet would I have it any different?"

His eyes showed her the anguish he was suffering.

He put out his arms and drew Cassandra from the chair.

"I love you!" he said. "I love you and I know that really nothing else matters. Will you be poor with me, my darling — for a few years at any rate?"

"You mean . . . ?"

"You will have no pretty gowns, no gaiety, just a rather dull life in a small house, but we shall be together."

He held her close in his arms. His eyes were looking into hers as if he was searching once again for something that was of the utmost importance to him.

Cassandra tried to speak but the words

would not come to her lips.

"I am asking you to marry me," the Duke said very softly. "What is your answer, my beloved?"

He saw the sudden light in her eyes and there was no need for words.

His mouth came down on to hers holding her captive.

"I love you . . ." she tried to say then he was kissing her wildly and it was impossible to speak.

Only inside herself Cassandra felt waves of happiness like white doves flying up to the Heavens.

She had won! He loved her!

He loved her enough to sacrifice everything that had mattered to him in the past.

He loved her and she felt his lips demanding her complete surrender.

No-one she thought, could know such happiness and not die of the wonder of it!

Chapter Nine

Cassandra shut her eyes so that Hannah, thinking she was asleep, would stop grumbling.

"I have never in all my life known such a carry on!" Hannah had exclaimed last night.

She said it not once but a dozen times when Cassandra had returned to Park Lane to inform the old maid that they were leaving for Yorkshire by the seven o'clock train the following morning.

"There's a good train, stopping only a few times, that leaves at nine-thirty," Hannah said.

"I know that," Cassandra answered, "but I wish to leave at seven. It you cannot be ready, Hannah, I will go alone and you can follow later."

She had known this was the surest way to make Hannah get the packing done and be sure that they left together.

Listening with her eyes closed to the rumble of the wheels on the track, Cassandra found herself re-living the wonder she had felt when she knew that the Duke loved her enough to give up his ancestral house so that they could be married.

She was well aware of the immensity of his sacrifice and how despite his complaints about being tied to the Alchester Estate, it was in fact a part of him, and to sell it would be like loosing an arm or a leg.

"Are you . . . sure?" she had asked him later.

They were seated together on the sofa so that he could still hold her in his arms.

"Sure that I want to marry you?" he asked. "I am more sure of it than I have been of anything else in my whole life."

"But we have . . . known each other such a . . . short time," Cassandra murmured.

"I feel that you have always been there in my heart," he answered. "The woman I have always been looking for, the wife I have wanted beside me, but whom I could never find."

There was a depth of sincerity in his voice that told Cassandra he spoke the truth.

"I love you!" he went on. "I love everything about you. Your absurdly red-gold hair, your little nose, your blue eyes! But more than all these I love the quickness of your brain and the kindness of your heart."

"You are . . . flattering me!" Cassandra demurred.

"I am telling you what I believe to be the truth," the Duke answered. "But I forgot to mention something else which I love."

"What is that?" she asked lifting her face a little to look up at him.

"Your lips!" he answered.

Then he was kissing her again and it was difficult to say anything more. . . .

A long time later Cassandra looked at the clock on the mantelpiece and realised it was time they returned to London.

It was then she could not help asking the question which had trembled on her lips for some time.

"What are you . . . going to do about . . . the girl you were supposed to . . . marry?"

The Duke rose from the sofa to stand with his back to her looking into the fire.

"I admit that in some ways I have been a cad," he said. "Our engagement should have been announced two years ago, but she was in mourning for her grandfather and we did not meet. Then, after my father's death, I decided to make it clear that I did not intend to go on with the arrangement he had made with the girl's father. But I was afraid —"

"Of what?"

"That my business commitments would fail and I should be left at the mercy of

Carwen! I had begun to find out the sort of swine he was."

The Duke paused to add:

"So I did nothing."

"And now?" Cassandra asked, her eyes on his broad shoulders and his head bent to look into the flames.

"I must behave decently," he said speaking as if to himself. "I will go to Yorkshire tomorrow and see Sir James Sherburn. After all, he was my father's greatest friend. If nothing else, I owe him a personal explanation."

"And what will that be?" Cassandra asked.

The Duke turned round.

"I shall tell him the truth," he said, "that I have fallen in love with someone so utterly adorable that not all the gold in the world could prevent me from marrying her!"

"He loves me!" Cassandra said to herself now. "He loves me! And everything I ever wanted or dreamed of in life has come true!"

At the same time she was aware of a real fear within herself that the Duke might be angry when he learned the truth.

She had known she could not confess her deception while they sat in front of the fire in the Library at Alchester Park.

It had also been impossible to do so when they had ridden back to London, arriving late at the stables of Alchester House where the Duke kept his horses.

The house was closed because he could not afford to live there, and in the stables, which could accommodate a dozen horses, there were only the pair which they had driven to the country.

The Duke saw them in their stalls and said to Cassandra:

"Your luggage will be waiting for you at the flat."

When Cassandra and the Duke arrived at Bury Street, it was in fact waiting for her in the Hall, and the Doorman had charge of her jewellery case.

"I was told to give it only into your own hands, Miss," he said.

"Shall I come upstairs with you?" the Duke asked.

"No," Cassandra answered. "I am tired and I am going straight to bed. Thank you for a wonderful day."

She put her hands in his and he raised them to his lips.

It was impossible to say more because the porter was within earshot.

The Duke had already promised as they rode towards London that he would return from Yorkshire on Wednesday and they would dine together that evening.

As soon as he had departed in his carriage in which they had driven from his stables to Jermyn Street, Cassandra asked the porter to find her a cab and place her luggage on it.

When he had done so she handed him the key of the flat.

"I shall not be returning," she said. "Here is the key and I should be grateful if you would get in touch with the Agent."

The porter thought it strange, but it was not for him to argue with the tenants.

As Cassandra drove away, she knew how glad she was that she would never again have to enter that horrible vulgar flat.

She wondered how she had ever allowed herself to rent such a place, but at the time she had not understood as much about the theatrical world as she did now.

As the train carried her home to Yorkshire it was a satisfaction in itself to know that she was going back to security, to her parents who loved her and had protected her, and cosseted her from the crude realities of the world outside her home.

She had never dreamt that there would be women who suffered as Nancy Wood had, or women who could flaunt the conventions like Lady McDonald, and in a different manner, Mrs. Langtry.

'I have learnt a lot,' Cassandra told herself.

But she knew her father would not consider it particularly desirable knowledge.

She was well aware that there was every likelihood of his being extremely angry at her behavior. But what was more important at this moment was what the Duke would say when she told him the truth.

'I will make him understand . . . he must understand!' Cassandra told herself.

She was conscious all the same, of a little quiver of fear and a number of questions in her mind which would not be silenced.

Now that she knew him, she was well aware that he would dislike being beholden to his wife as much as he had resented being beholden to his father and Lord Carwen.

He was a strong character and to a man who was as masculine as he was, it would be humiliating to know that his wife held the purse-strings.

Then Cassandra told herself it was only a question of time. The Duke had said that eventually he would be rich in his own right and she was sure he would be.

She had never yet heard him exaggerate or boast about anything, and he had been absolutely certain in his own mind that in perhaps only a few years the investments he had made in Australia and South Africa would bring him the fortune he so ardently desired.

Yet at the moment the house had to go, and that he should be willing to sell Alchester Park with the whole history of his family behind it because he loved her was to Cassandra so perfect, so utterly marvellous that she could only pray that she herself would be worthy of such a love.

She loved him so overwhelmingly that she thought now that, if he had in fact been in love with anyone else, she would not have wished to go on living.

She loved everything about him — not only his outstanding good looks but his air of authority, his charm, his pride and his sense of humour.

Because she was jealous she could not help saying to him:

"You must have . . . spent a lot of . . . money on the pretty . . . ladies from the Gaiety?"

"Are you suspecting diamonds?" the Duke asked.

His eyes twinkled.

"Dare I be conceited enough to tell you that I did not have to give anything more expensive than a few flowers for any favors I received?"

He had kissed her and added:

"That at least is one economy I can make in the future!"

Cassandra had sent a telegram first thing in the morning to The Towers to say that she and Hannah were arriving at York at 2.00. P.M.

It was nearly an hour's drive to her home, and she knew that, even travelling by the faster train, it would be impossible for the Duke to arrive until after five thirty.

That would give her time to prepare her father for the shock of what he had come to say.

But in her own mind Cassandra was not decided as to how she would let him learn the truth.

She somehow felt desperately shy at the thought of just letting him walk in and find her there.

The carriage was waiting at York Station and all the way to The Towers Cassandra was very quiet.

She was thinking apprehensively of what lay ahead, and though Hannah tried to talk she only answered in monosyllables.

The Butler was at the door to greet her.

"Welcome home, Miss Cassandra."

"Is Sir James in?" Cassandra asked as she walked into the Hall.

"No, Miss, Sir James and Her Ladyship had left before your telegram arrived."

"Then my father did not know I was coming back?"

"No, Miss. Sir James and Her Ladyship were having luncheon with Lord Harrogate and going on afterwards to a Reception given by the Archbishop of York."

"Of course!" Cassandra explained. "I remember that engagement."

She also had been invited.

"Sir James has ordered dinner a little later than usual," the Butler went on, "but he and Her Ladyship should be back before seven o'clock."

"Is there another telegram?" Cassandra asked.

"Yes, Miss. It also arrived after Sir James had left, so I opened it, as he has always instructed me to do."

"What did it say?"

"It is from the Duke of Alchester, Miss Cassandra, to say he is arriving by the train which reaches York at three twenty-five. I have arranged for a carriage to meet him."

Cassandra considered a moment.

"Now listen, Hudson," she said. "When His Grace arrives I want you to inform him that Sir James is unfortunately not here to greet him and that as I have a bad cold I will receive him in my Sitting-room. Is that clear?"

"Yes, Miss Cassandra."

"Just show him into the room and do not interrupt us until I ring."

"Very good, Miss."

The Butler looked slightly surprised at the instructions, but Cassandra knew he was too well-trained not to carry them out.

She then ran up the stairs to her own room — she had a lot of preparations to make.

The train must have been late because although Cassandra was ready and waiting by half past four, it was after five o'clock when she heard footsteps coming along the corridor towards her Sitting-room.

Although it was not yet dark outside she had drawn the curtains and there was a fire in the grate, the flames flickering over wood logs.

She had put a screen around an arm-chair which had its back to the windows as if to furnish protection against draughts, and she had extinguished all the lights in the room with the exception of one cut-glass oil-lamp.

It stood on the circular table in the centre of the room and on the table Cassandra had laid the two Albums she had treasured for so many years.

Because she was determined to keep her secret a surprise until the last possible moment, she wore a pair of dark glasses and held a fan in one hand as if to protect her face from the heat of the flames.

She knew it would be difficult for the Duke, coming from the light in the rest of the house into the dimness of the room, to recognise her at first sight.

She also had the feeling that because he would be embarrassed at what he had to say, he would not look at her very closely.

'It will be a surprise — a wonderful surprise for him when he knows who I am!' she told herself.

But her words sounded more convincing than the feeling they evoked within her. She was still afraid he might be angry!

It seemed to her while she waited that every moment was a century of time.

The clock ticking softly on the mantelpiece seemed to pause between every second.

Her heart was beating feverishly in her breast, and she kept moistening her lips because they were dry.

"Why should I be afraid?" she asked herself, and yet she knew she was.

Cassandra began to fear that something had gone wrong and that the Duke had missed the train.

Perhaps, she thought, he was trying to get in touch with her in London.

Then at last she heard the door open.

"His Grace, the Duke of Alchester," Hudson announced.

Cassandra felt herself tremble as the Duke walked across the room towards her.

He put something down on the table by the lamp, then he came nearer to the fire.

"I hear you have a cold," he said courteously. "I am sorry if you stayed up to receive me when you should have been in bed."

"It is . . . not too . . . bad," Cassandra managed to say.

She had intended to sound hoarse, but there was really little need to disguise her voice because she was so nervous it sounded strange even to herself.

The Duke did not look at her.

He stood for a moment holding out his hands to the flames. Then he said in what seemed to Cassandra a hard voice:

"I intended to speak to your father, but as he is not here perhaps we can speak frankly with each other?"

It was a question.

Cassandra managed to murmur:

"Y . . . yes."

"Then I think you know why I am here," the Duke said, "and what was arranged between your father and mine before he died? Their plan was that we should be married."

He paused, Cassandra said nothing and after a moment he went on:

"So, Miss Sherburn, let me put it very simply — I shall be deeply honored if you will consent to be my wife!"

Cassandra was frozen into immobility.

She could not believe that what she had heard was not a product of her imagination.

He could not have said it! He could not!

Then through her dark glasses she looked at his profile clear in the light of the fire, and saw the square, determined set of his chin and the hard line of his mouth.

He meant it! He had said it and he meant it!

He had changed his mind after she had left him yesterday and decided that love was not worth the sacrifice of his heritage, of the house which had meant so much in the history of his family.

It was impossible for her to speak or to move.

She could only stare at the Duke as the

tears began to run from her eyes down her cheeks, and her hand which still held the fan to shadow her face trembled.

She felt as if the whole ceiling had crashed on to her head; that everything she had ever believed in had fallen in pieces around her.

And now the numbness of her body was replaced with an agony that was like a thousand knives being driven into her heart.

The Duke turned towards her.

"Come," he said. "I have something to show you."

He put out his hand as he spoke and taking hers he drew her unresisting from the chair in which she had been sitting across the room towards the table.

She went with him because he compelled her and because she was quite incapable of speech.

They reached the table and Cassandra saw there was now a magazine lying beside the two Albums.

"I want you to look at this," the Duke said. "Perhaps you would be able to see more clearly without those glasses."

He took them off as he spoke and now with her heart palpitating Cassandra tried to understand what was happening; tried to look at what lay on the table in front of her.

It was a copy of "*The Sporting and Dra-*

matic" and on the open page there was a portrait sketch of herself!

Although it had been copied from the photograph which had been taken by the photographer in York which her father had disliked, it was quite unmistakable.

Underneath it was written:

"A NOTABLE LADY RIDER TO HOUNDS AND BELLE OF THE YORKSHIRE BALLS — MISS CASSANDRA SHERBURN."

She stood looking at it and the Duke said:

"I could hardly fail to recognise you, could I?"

His voice was harsh and now Cassandra managed to say through dry lips:

"I . . . could not . . . tell you . . . yesterday . . ."

"Why not?" the Duke asked in an uncompromising tone, "or need I ask such a foolish question? You wished to extort from me the last vestige of humiliation — to force me down on my knees in front of you."

"No . . . No!" Cassandra whispered. "It was not like . . . that."

"Of course it was," the Duke retorted. "Do not deceive me any further. Not content with my title — you wanted my heart also. It was very clever!"

"No! No!" Cassandra cried again. "I . . ."

"You were determined to manipulate me," he interrupted, "as I have been manipulated all my life. First by my father, then by Carwen and now by you. Well, you have been most successful, and I can only congratulate you on being an even better actress than you pretended to be!"

His voice cut like a whip and Cassandra cried frantically:

"You must listen to me . . . you must! It was nothing like . . . that . . . look, I have . . . these to show you."

She threw open the Albums as she spoke.

The Duke looked down at the newspaper cuttings stuck neatly in the pages, but the expression on his face did not change.

"There is . . . something . . . else," Cassandra said.

She ran across the room to her writing-desk.

With hands which trembled so much that she could hardly control them she found the key of the secret drawer, opened it and drew out her diary.

Then she went back to the Duke.

He had not moved from the table. He still stood there with the two open Albums and her picture in front of him.

There was nothing in the Diary after the last entry written on March 29th, which she had made before she left for London.

She held it out to the Duke.

"Read this . . . read . . . it," she begged.

The Duke did not look at her and she thought for one moment he would refuse to take the Diary from her.

Then he took the little book and held it towards the light, so that he could see better.

In Cassandra's neat and elegant handwriting he saw written:

"Papa has just told me that after all this time he has received a letter from the Duke of Alchester.

I had been certain, since his father's death, that the young Duke had changed his mind about the arrangements that were made so long ago for our marriage. Now because I understand he is desperately hard-up, he is prepared to go through with it.

"But I know this is something I cannot and will not do! It has been Papa's dream that I should marry the son of his old friend and that also I should be a Duchess.

"If we had become engaged two years

ago when I was only seventeen-and-a-half, I should have accepted Papa's judgment in this as I have done in so many other things.

"But now I am older and I know that it would be a travesty of everything in which I believe and which I hold sacred for me to marry a man I love but who, I am convinced loves someone else.

"I had also thought because I have loved him so deeply ever since I was twelve years old and saw him at the Eton and Harrow cricket match, that he would come to love me and that we could find happiness together.

"But I know now that was merely a child's dream.

"My love for him has prevented me from marrying anyone else or caring for any of the men who have proposed to me.

"But I would rather be an old-maid and remain unmarried for the whole of my life than suffer the humiliation and degradation of being married to the Duke who wants only my money.

"I am certain it would be easier to marry, if I must, someone for whom I have no affection, rather than to know that Varro kissed me and touched me because it was his duty. That I could not face.

"In fact I would rather die than be tortured by my longing for something very different.

"I wanted to tell Papa this but then I thought he would merely brush my arguments aside unless I can prove irrefutably that the Duke is in love with someone else.

"I am sure he is, and that she is an actress from the Gaiety Theatre. But because he would not be likely to admit it to Papa, I have to find out the truth for myself.

"I have therefore decided that I shall go to London and try to meet the Duke through Mrs. Langtry. I shall pretend to be a part of the world which he enjoys and which obviously means so much to him.

"People have always said I look theatrical. If I can act the part of an actress sufficiently well to convince him, I can I feel sure, find out the truth.

"There are other heiresses in the world who would be only too willing to give him their money in exchange for his coronet, but all these years it has not mattered to me whether he was a Duke or a pauper.

"I have loved him because the first time I saw him I lost my heart!

"It sounds so stupid put down on

paper, but that is what happened.

"Now I must find out the truth and I will then tell Papa that I cannot marry the Duke. He will not force me in those circumstances.

"But I know that however long I live, even if I never see him again, I shall never love anyone as I love Varro."

The Duke reached the bottom of the page.

Then as he stared at what he had read with an almost incredulous look in his eyes, a very low, broken voice said behind him:

"You are . . . not on your . . . knees, Varro . . . I am! Please . . . please . . . will you . . . marry me? I love you so . . . desperately."

The Duke turned round slowly, Cassandra was kneeling on the floor behind him.

Her hands were clasped together, she had thrown back her head to look up at him and the tears were streaming down her cheeks.

She looked into his eyes, and seeing no softening in the hardness of his expression, she gave a pitiful little sob as she whispered:

"If you . . . will not . . . marry . . . me will you make . . . me your . . . mistress?"

For a moment the Duke was still. Then he bent down and putting his arms around

Cassandra pulled her roughly against him.

"How dare you say such a thing?" he asked and his voice was still angry.

But as if he could not help himself, his mouth sought hers.

For a moment his lips were hard and rough.

Then as he felt her body soft and yielding against his and as he knew that a flame had been ignited in them both, his kiss became more tender and at the same time more demanding.

It seemed to Cassandra that the room whirled around her and she was dizzy with the wonder of it.

Then the Duke was kissing the tears from her cheeks, her wet eyes and again her mouth with a passion that made her quiver and tremble.

Yet her whole being responded to the fire that consumed him.

When finally he raised his head to look down at her she turned her face and hid it against his shoulder.

"I am . . . sorry," she whispered.

"How could you have done anything so crazy, so reprehensible, so incredibly naughty?" he asked.

She did not answer and he went on:

"God knows in what sort of trouble you

might have found yourself, if I had not been there to protect you."

"But you were . . . there!" she murmured. "And I . . . had to find . . . out the . . . truth."

"There would have been better ways of doing it than acting a part though having no conception whatever of the type of woman you were pretending to be."

"You . . . were . . . deceived!"

"I was completely bewildered," the Duke replied. "I fell in love with you when you were shocked by the 'Can-Can' that first evening at Carwen's house, but I could not understand what was happening. How anyone who looked as you looked with your painted face could be so innocent and so obviously ignorant of the world was beyond my comprehension!"

"I . . . thought I was rather . . . clever!" Cassandra murmured.

"As a performance it was lamentable! And let me tell you another thing: if I ever catch you reddening your lips again, I will beat you! Do you understand?"

He held her very closely against him, and Cassandra said in a small hesitating voice:

"Does that . . . mean that . . . you are . . . going to marry me?"

He looked down into her eyes and there was a smile on his lips.

"I suppose I shall have to!" he said. "After all, the fact that you slept in my suite is extremely compromising."

"I locked . . . the door."

The Duke laughed.

"Because I told you to! Oh, my darling, when I think of how badly you have behaved and what wild, crazy chances you have taken, I am appalled! It terrifies me even now to think of what might have happened to you!"

"I knew I was . . . safe with . . . you."

"You will always be safe with me in the future," the Duke said firmly, "for the simple reason that I shall never let you out of my sight! How could I, when you are so ridiculously lovely? But I am going to punish you because you have deceived me and because you have behaved so badly."

"How?" Cassandra asked rather apprehensively.

"We are going to be married almost immediately," he said, "but you are not going to have the pleasure of flaunting yourself in London as the lovely young Duchess of Alchester. We are going on a very long honeymoon trip first to Australia and then to South Africa."

"How wonderful!" Cassandra cried, her face radiant with happiness.

"When we return," the Duke went on, "I anticipate it will be time to put our house in order for the future generations."

For a moment Cassandra did not understand his meaning, then she blushed.

"You mean . . ." she began and hesitated.

"I mean exactly what you think I mean," the Duke answered, "and how, when you blush like that, you ever expected anyone to think of you as a hard-boiled, tough little actress, I do not know!"

He kissed her again.

"I love you!" he said after a moment. "I love you so much that I can think of nothing but you."

"That is what I have felt about . . . you for years."

"Have you really been in love with me for so long?" he asked wonderingly.

"Ever since I last saw you," Cassandra answered. "I felt we were meant for each other. Did you not feel the same?"

"I thought it from the first moment I set eyes on you at Carwen's party," the Duke confessed. "I was depressed, worried and very apprehensive about the future. "Then I saw you standing in front of me and everything was changed from that moment."

"And nothing else . . . matters?" Cassandra asked.

He saw the meaning in her eyes and knew what she asked.

"Nothing, my precious," he said. "Titles, money, rank are unimportant compared with a love like ours! A love which will last all through our lives."

"I love . . . you!" Cassandra whispered. "I love you . . . agonizingly."

Then the Duke's lips were on hers fiercely, passionately demanding they asked her complete and absolute surrender.

She knew he would always be her Master and gloried in his strength.

She felt that he swept her away into a sunlit, perfect world where there was only themselves.

He raised his head.

"Do . . . you really . . . love me?" she whispered.

"I worship you — my wonderful darling."

"For . . . ever?"

"For eternity and beyond."

Cassandra gave a sigh of sheer happiness, then the Duke's lips blotted out thought.

She could only thrill and thrill at the rapture and ecstasy of a love which was part of the Divine.